the summer i learned to fly

the summer i learned to fly

Dana Reinhardt

WENDY
LAMB
BOOKS

Text copyright © 2011 by Dana Reinhardt
Jacket art copyright © 2011 by Ericka O'Rourke

All rights reserved. Published in the United States by
Wendy Lamb Books,
an imprint of Random House Children's Books,
a division of Random House, Inc., New York.

Wendy Lamb Books and the colophon are
trademarks of Random House, Inc.

Visit us on the Web! www.randomhouse.com/teens

Educators and librarians, for a variety of teaching tools, visit us at
www.randomhouse.com/teachers

Library of Congress Cataloging-in-Publication Data
Reinhardt, Dana.
The summer I learned to fly / Dana Reinhardt. — 1st ed.
p. cm.
ISBN 978-0-385-73954-2 (trade) — ISBN 978-0-385-90792-7
(lib. bdg.) — ISBN 978-0-375-89787-0 (ebook) —
ISBN 978-0-385-73955-9 (pbk.) [1. Interpersonal relations—Fiction.
2. Single-parent families—Fiction. 3. Stores, Retail—Fiction. 4. Rats as
pets—Fiction. 5. Family life—California—Fiction. 6. California—History—
Fiction.] I. Title.
PZ7.R2758Sum 2011
[Fic]—dc22
2010029412

Printed in the United States of America

10 9 8 7 6 5 4 3

First Edition

To Wendy Lamb and Douglas Stewart,
for believing

the grand opening

For some people it's the smell of sunblock. Or pine trees. A burnt marshmallow from the embers of a campfire. Maybe your grandfather's aftershave.

Everyone has that smell. The particular scent that transports you, even if only for an instant, to the long-ago, faraway land of your childhood.

For me, it's the smell of Limburger. Or Camembert. Sometimes Stilton. Take your pick from the stinkiest of cheeses.

My mother's shop was on Euclid Avenue. But believe me, it's not the Euclid Avenue you know now, with thirty-dollar manicures and stores that sell nothing but fancy soap in paisley paper.

Back then Euclid Avenue was the kind of place where a kid like me could find something to spend fifty cents on. And I did, almost every day, at Fireside Liquor. It was the summer of 1986 and I wasn't buying alcohol; I was only thirteen. But fifty cents bought me a Good News: peanuts, caramel, chocolate. The red label declared it *Hawaii's Favorite* candy bar, an odd claim, but one that made it seem, and even taste, exotic.

I'd never been to Hawaii. I'd never been anywhere to speak of. We didn't have much money, only what we got from Dad's life insurance policy, and what we did have had all gone into the Cheese Shop.

That's what it was called. The Cheese Shop. No stroke of brilliance in the creativity department, but the name said what it needed to say: Come inside and you'll find cheese. Any sort you can imagine.

On the day we opened, Mrs. Mutchnick, who owned the fabric store across the street, a grandmotherly type with her hair barely holding on to its ever-present bun, brought over a gift. It was a most unexpected opening-day gift. Not flowers. Not champagne. And I couldn't possibly have guessed when I unwrapped it (because Mrs. Mutchnick presented it to me) that this gift would come to change my life.

But I'm getting ahead of myself.

First, there was the issue of the health inspection.

There are basic requirements. Things one must do in order to open a store that sells food.

Keep your shop clean. I mean truly clean, not what you try to pass off when your mom looks at your room, with everything shoved in a drawer or under your bed. You must keep your establishment absolutely spotless.

Have running water, hot and cold, and a working restroom.

Your freezer must be a certain temperature, which is different from the temperature you must keep the refrigerated cheese cases, which is different from the temperature you must keep the shop itself.

And generally, things need to smell good, which is easy enough, unless you happen to be in the business of selling stinky cheeses.

This is precisely where we ran into trouble with the inspector.

He'd enter the shop nose first, as if it, and not his pea-sized brain, were in charge of the rest of him. He came around often, too often, in the days leading up to the opening, rapping his clipboard on the shop front window and doing a little wave with his spindly fingers.

His name was Fletcher Melcher. I know it sounds like I'm making that up, but I'm not. And I'm not making up the forest of hair that lived in each of his nostrils either.

We called him Retcher Belcher, about as inspired as calling Mom's store the Cheese Shop, and he almost succeeded in keeping the shop from opening, which seemed to be his very purpose for walking the planet.

The day before we were to sell our first wedge of cheese, the freezer decided to stop working. And who should arrive only moments after we'd realized this? Right. The Belcher.

I'd taken the bus to the shop. Mom had arranged for me to ride a new bus from school, one that took me to the vicinity of the store rather than our small house not far from the beach. Nobody talked to me on this new bus, but that wasn't much of a change from what it was like to ride the old bus.

I was coming from Fireside Liquor, about to open my Good News, and I could see through the storefront window that Mom was in a state.

She was all flailing limbs. Her usually short and spiky hair had taken on that puffy look it got when she ran her fingers through it obsessively. She was yelling at Nick while he stood by and took it calmly, as only someone in possession of two particular qualities could.

One: Nick was unflappable. Some people would attribute this to the proximity of Fireside Liquor. But Nick wasn't a drunk; he was a surfer, just turned nineteen. Mellow to the max.

Two: Even if he knew almost nothing about cheese, Nick could fix practically anything.

The bell jingled as I walked through the front door. A sound that would later come to drive me mad.

"Drew," he said, and he put both of his hands on my shoulders. He fixed his green, sea-glass eyes on mine. "Thank God you're here."

His third outstanding quality: Nick Drummond was impossibly good-looking.

"Get your old lady under control, will you? Take her outside for some fresh air. Or maybe even a smoke." And with that he disappeared into the freezer.

This was Nick's stab at humor. Mom didn't smoke. Except for her love of cheese, she was pretty much a health nut. She did yoga. She meditated. She wore an earthy-smelling perfume, except when she was at work, because Mom believed that nothing should interfere with a customer's right to freely whiff the cheese.

"We're up a creek," she said.

"Chill out, Mom. It's gonna be cool." I'd only known

Nick about a month, since we'd started getting the shop ready to open, but I was already perfecting his lingo. Anything to make him notice me.

"No, Drew. It's not *gonna be cool*. Fletcher Melcher is on his way. Daisy called. He's just asked for his check."

Daisy owned the diner three blocks up. That the Belcher was taking his lunch there could only mean one thing: he was on his way to us. He had it in for Mom and the shop, and every merchant on Euclid Avenue knew it.

"Nick'll take care of it," I told her. "He can do anything."

Mom reached over and stroked my hair. She smiled at me wistfully. "Oh Birdie, you're too sweet."

She walked behind the counter, grabbed an oversize wheel of Jarlsberg, and cut us each a slice. A disconcerting clanging came from inside the walk-in freezer. Mom winced. I pointed to the slice in her hand, then pointed to her mouth. She took a bite.

Jarlsberg: the comfort cheese.

As predicted, the rapping of the Belcher's clipboard on the front window followed. As did his little wave. Mom reluctantly motioned him inside.

He stuck that nose of his into the air and made a beeline for the cheese case's thermostat. Forty-four degrees. Perfect.

He walked around the back of the counter. Ran his fingertip along the butcher block. Checked the sink. The hand soap. Slithered his way past the shelves of crackers and jars of olives, toward the back office and the ill-fated walk-in freezer.

He reached for the handle and jumped back as the door

5

seemed to open itself. There stood Nick in one of the parkas we kept nearby for anyone who had to spend a stretch of time inside the freezer shelving sauces or lasagnas, ravioli or chicken pot pies, the things we sold other than cheese, because nobody, not even Mom, could live on cheese alone.

Nick smiled, his cheeks red with cold. He looked like he'd just gotten off a chairlift at the top of a snow-covered mountain on a gloriously sunny day.

The Belcher pushed past him. He checked the thermostat, grudgingly nodded, and moved on to the employee restroom.

Mom shot Nick a thumbs-up. He did an extravagant bow.

When Fletcher Melcher finally took his leave, Nick told us that he hadn't fixed the freezer; he'd only messed with the thermostat. So back on went the parka, and back went Nick into what was left of the cold, and thirty minutes later the freezer was working again, and sixteen hours later we were officially in business, because Nick Drummond was nothing short of a miracle.

And later the next evening, when we had our grand opening party, with platters of cheese and wine in plastic cups, Mom wandering through the crowd receiving hugs and flowers and unsolicited advice, Mrs. Mutchnick closed up her fabric store and crossed Euclid Avenue with a gift.

It was wrapped in a piece of striped fabric, tied loosely on the top with twine.

What a clever gift, she'd thought. *Perfect for someone in the business of selling cheese.* She didn't have to go any farther than four blocks to Pacific Pets and Pet Supply to buy it.

She brought it right over to me, though she'd intended to

6

give it to Mom. She gave it to me, she said, because I looked lonely.

I looked like I needed a friend.

"You might want to open it now, dear."

I untied the twine. Inside that striped fabric wrapping was a small wire cage, and inside that small wire cage was a rat.

He was an ordinary rat. He didn't talk. He didn't have magical powers, a lesson to teach me, or wisdom to impart. He was just a rat, and although at first he made me squeamish, I grew to love him terribly.

But that isn't why he changed my life.

It was because this rat, black with a white belly and whiskers too long for his small face, one afternoon escaped his wire cage, and led me to a boy named Emmett Crane.

a note about names

I named him Humboldt Fog, after my favorite cheese, and though certain occasions called for the use of his proper name, His Excellency the Lord High Rat Humboldt Fog, he came to be known simply as Hum.

And since I'm bothering to explain his name, I guess I should say a word or two about mine.

Drew is not my real name.

I came into the world as Robin. Which accounted for why my mother still called me Birdie, and it was my misfortune that she often called me Birdie in front of Nick Drummond.

Robin Drew Solo.

That's my real name. My father's name was Drew, and I guess I would have been Drew too had I been a boy, but obviously I wasn't, so I was named Robin after some long-lost relative nobody seemed to know or care much about.

Then my father died. I was only three. And from the black hole of her grief Mom couldn't let go of that name. She changed my name so she could hear herself say his, countless times a day.

Eventually she did the paperwork and saw to it officially—and well after the fact of my birth—that despite being a girl, I be called after my father.

So I became Drew Robin Solo. Sometimes Birdie. Except for Emmett Crane, who was the only person in my life, then or since, who chose to call me Robin.

the book of lists

I found it one day while looking for a shawl. I'd never seen Mom wear a shawl, so I had no reason to think I'd find one in her messy closet, but I figured it didn't hurt to look.

Shawls had replaced the hooded sweatshirts we all tied around our waists for the first half of the school year. Now it was all about knit woolen shawls, triangular in shape, so that the longest point conveniently covered your butt. That we lived in California, and that these were some of our hotter months, didn't seem to matter at all. Like most of the kids my age, particularly the girls, fads were unpredictable and irrational.

I had to have one. And since the shop was still very new, and what we might have had to spend on something like a shawl had gone instead toward a hot-seal plastic wrapper for wedges of cheese, I went looking in Mom's closet.

I never did find a shawl. Or anything with which to cover my butt. I found something so much better.

I found it under a pile of balled-up sweaters, which I figured hadn't been touched for years, not only because I'd never seen them (I paid close attention to Mom's fashion choices), and not only because they stank of must, but also because Mom wasn't a tall woman. And the shelf that held them was up high. Too high for an ordinary chair. So high that I had to get the ladder from the garage to reach that shelf, and the ladder spit out rust as I creaked it open.

After holding up and then rejecting each musty sweater, I came to the bottom of the pile, where I found a composition notebook with a cover like TV static. The spaces for a name and subject were left blank, so I assumed the inside would be blank too.

But then I opened it.

I didn't recognize the handwriting. It wasn't Mom's soft precise cursive, which I tried so hard to mimic. It was small and tight. Blocky. Leaning to the left. The handwriting of a man.

The handwriting of my dead father.

What other reasonable choice did I have but to re-ball Mom's sweaters and return them to the too-high shelf? To refold the metal ladder and return it to the garage? To take that composition book to my room, sit down on my floor, and begin to read?

Lists.

It was a book of lists from my father. Lists of everything from favorite foods (*lobster*) to least-favorite bands of all time (*The Doors*). His favorite season: *winter, the real kind.* Favorite place: *San Francisco, at the break of day.* Regrets: *not taking up the motorcycle before it became a pathetic cliché.* Embarrassing moments: *dinner at the home of my girlfriend's parents, clogged toilet.*

I read that composition book from cover to cover sitting on my pink shag carpet, but I didn't stop there. I read it most days. I returned to it like some people return to the Bible. And like the Bible, there were days I needed it more than others.

It's hard to say whether there was something that struck me the hardest or surprised me the most. When you don't know someone, everything you learn about him is its own sort of surprise. But I can say what it was I read that first afternoon that lodged itself inside me like a feather, so that only holding my breath would stop the fluttery, slightly sickening feeling.

Fears: *that I'll never see my Birdie learn to fly.*

throwing caution to the wind

Nick Drummond drove a lime-green Vespa. One afternoon, just before school let out for the summer, I was getting off the bus when he pulled up to the curb and flashed his signature grin.

"Need a lift?"

I was born cautious. I never liked roller coasters or scary movies. I thought the girls who smoked cigarettes outside the minimart looked foolish, like kids who walk around in their mothers' high heels.

I made every choice carefully. Until the afternoon Nick Drummond pulled up on his lime-green Vespa and offered me a ride, and without hesitating, for fear he might change his mind and speed off without me, I said yes.

We were only three blocks from the shop, so I didn't need a ride. Need wasn't the point.

He never wore a helmet, so he didn't have one to offer me, and even this didn't give my careful heart pause, because without a helmet, somebody might actually know it was me riding around on the back of Nick Drummond's Vespa.

I glanced over my shoulder at the school bus, but it was already departing. We took off in the wrong direction.

"I'm not due at the shop for half an hour," he shouted over his shoulder. "Let's go for a spin."

I grabbed tighter to his waist. His shaggy golden hair whipped me in the cheek, a strand catching in my mouth. We rode all the way to the coast and then arced north.

He took one hand off the handlebars. I didn't panic. He pointed to the ocean. "Check out those barrels!"

I had a vague sense this had something to do with surfing, but I wasn't totally sure.

I shouted back, "Cool!"

Nick had graduated from high school the summer before and was taking a few classes at the community college. He'd had a job pumping gas until he came across Mom's ad in the newspaper. Now when he wasn't in the Cheese Shop or at school learning mechanical engineering, he could always be found at the beach. He smelled like the sea.

Nick's mother had followed a man she met in a bar all the way to Argentina and never come back. She'd left Nick the apartment, a year's worth of rent, and her old Vespa. He'd been taking care of himself since age sixteen, and from what I could tell he was doing a bang-up job.

He was Mom's first hire and she adored him. She wanted more for him than his current existence. She wanted him to go to a real college. Get more serious. Stop wasting his natural talents. Come fall, she'd harass him daily to fill out applications to schools he couldn't possibly afford, especially after everything he'd been through, but that was still a ways off.

On this early June afternoon I could count the days until summer vacation on one hand. Other kids had plans for sleepaway camp in the High Sierras, or visits to grandparents in far-off towns, maybe a local class in oil painting or photography.

Not me.

I had a job lined up at the shop. I'd sweep floors and wipe countertops. Take out the trash. Wash windows. Sometimes I'd even have to stock the walk-in freezer. And I couldn't imagine anything more perfect.

As Nick fishtailed his Vespa, bringing it to a screeching halt, I couldn't help thinking that he was showing off. (*Showing off for me!*) I grabbed on tighter and buried my face in his back. I also couldn't help thinking that maybe this was how I would meet my end, with my arms around Nick Drummond's waist, and I guessed that there might be worse ways to go.

He turned off the engine. I released him finally and caught my breath. Only then did I think of Hum.

He was where I always kept him: in my backpack. Inside his wire cage. I'd stopped carrying my books in my bag and had lined the bottom with rags and old T-shirts so he wouldn't knock around too much. Inside his cage I'd put a sock with the toes cut off that he liked to burrow his way through and a few macadamia nuts in the shell, his favorite snack. I took my books to school in a brown paper shopping bag, but school was almost over, and I didn't have much use for books anymore.

I undid the zipper, carefully lifted out Hum's cage, and peered through the wire mesh.

"Hum?"

Rats can't vomit, but I didn't know that yet. I'd learn it later, as I came to know everything about rats. So when I took Hum from my pack after this wild ride up the coast and back again, I expected to find him coated in his own sick.

Instead I found a rat, dead asleep.

I glanced up to see Nick entering the shop. He'd left me in the parking lot alone with my rat and my unnecessary worry, and this struck me as the cruel and inevitable part of loving someone like Nick Drummond from a distance. To him I was only a kid with unnecessary worries.

I returned Hum's cage to my bag and zipped it shut. Mom didn't know I took Hum with me everywhere, and she certainly didn't know that he accompanied me to the Cheese Shop in the afternoons after school. I'd never looked in the large spiral notebook that contained the county health code, but I was pretty sure it said something about not keeping a rat in your store.

My face was still flushed from the ride. From my sudden lack of caution. From my fear about Hum. From the taste of Nick's golden hair in my mouth.

I knew this all showed. My face didn't know how to keep secrets.

I found Mom sitting at the desk in the back room, furiously punching numbers into a calculator. A long ribbon of paper spilled down to the floor, tangling around the legs of her chair.

She reached out without looking up and touched my windswept hair.

"Hiya, Birdie," she said. "How was the day?"

I opened my mouth, but then the front door jingled, someone wandered in for a wedge of St. Nectaire, and Mom didn't stick around for my answer.

swoozie

She came from Wisconsin, the state famous for its cheese.

I'd decided that Wisconsin, in addition to dairy farming, must be in the business of growing the largest breasts known to humanity, because Swoozie had a major pair.

I had nothing to show for myself yet, not that I was in such a hurry, but breasts were very much on my thirteen-year-old mind. Most of the girls in my class were wearing bras, and complaining about it in a way that sounded suspiciously like bragging.

I was hoping that when my time came, I might split the difference someplace between Swoozie and my mother.

Swoozie was freckled and doughy, a year older than Mom, going through a divorce. She had no kids.

"I came out West to start over, to reinvent myself, to get away from my Wisconsin roots," she liked to say, although not so far away from those roots that she steered clear of cheese.

She hugged me when she saw me. Every time. They were the sorts of embraces others might reserve for people they hadn't seen in ages. She'd push my hair back from my face and say, "Tell your aunt Swoozie something she doesn't already know."

She was the type who took the role of aunt seriously. It's how she got her name, from a nephew who couldn't pronounce "Susie," and she had a fattened wallet filled with pictures of the freckled, doughy nieces and nephews she'd left behind in Wisconsin. I was the only youngish person she knew in her new life, and so I received the full bounty of her auntlike energy.

Swoozie fancied herself a matchmaker. Her own failed marriage inspired her to find love for others, and this annoyed me because I had no interest in watching Mom or Nick Drummond fall in love, and they were her two primary targets.

There were men who came in regularly, twice a week or more, and engaged Mom in long discussions about soft French cheeses versus Italian ones. The difference between virgin and extra-virgin olive oils. They'd talk wines too, and mom would write a list of recommendations they could take next door to Fireside Liquor. I thought they were just men who loved food, but Swoozie insisted they came to catch a glimpse of the "Cheese Babe."

It was hard for me to see Mom as anything but devoted to cheese and to me. As far as I knew, and I liked to think I *knew*, she hadn't dated anyone since my dad died.

And Nick, well, I was pretty sure Nick didn't need any help from Swoozie when it came to girls, but that didn't stop her from pointing out the cute ones. Especially as summer approached. Cute girls were everywhere, wearing spaghetti-strapped sundresses, sometimes even less.

I found Swoozie easy to talk to. We'd sit in the freezer where nobody could hear us, and while she shelved sauces I'd hold Hum on my lap and feed him ice chips. She kept Hum's visits to the shop a secret. It was understood that if Mom ever caught me I'd take full responsibility. I'd never throw Swoozie under the bus. We trusted each other.

I'd ask her about the things I couldn't ask anyone else. Like, for example: What's a Fu Manchu?

That came from the List of Biggest Mistakes. I never asked Mom about anything from Dad's Book of Lists because it made her too sad to talk about Dad. And there was the fact that Mom didn't know I'd stolen Dad's book, or that I kept it under my mattress, and that on more nights than not, I'd read from it with a flashlight, under my hand-stitched quilt, before going to sleep.

"A Fu Manchu is a mustache," Swoozie told me. "A very thin, unfortunate-looking mustache." I imagined it was especially unfortunate on a redheaded Irishman like my father.

I asked her about things like Geraldine Moore, a girl in the eighth grade who was two inches shorter than me and wore black eyeliner and cork-soled sandals. I'd heard something about her sneaking into the boys' bathroom with Doug Jensen, Peter Mason, and Eric Strauss. I wasn't totally certain what this was about, but I was supposed to know. Everybody knew. And I learned to nod and sigh like I got it, which I totally did not.

"Oh, Bird-girl," Swoozie would say. "Junior high is a

strange land inhabited by strange creatures. The best you can do is keep your head down and your nose clean, and hold your breath till college."

This pretty well summed up what I was already doing. Waiting. For what, exactly, I wasn't sure.

All I knew was that nothing ever happened to me, at least nothing that counted. Nothing mattered to me in the way cheese mattered to Mom. Or surfing to Nick. I was holding my breath, waiting for my life to begin.

I wouldn't, as it turned out, have to hold it too much longer.

friends: a history

It's not like I didn't have friends. I did. It's just that I preferred the company of Swoozie and Nick to pretty much anybody else on the planet.

I know how that sounds, like I was one of those kids who didn't know how to talk to her peers. Whose jokes fell flat. Who never wore the right clothes or listened to the right music. But I'd always had friends.

I can prove it:

Stephania Allessio.
Born three weeks after me in a house two doors away. We moved after my dad died, and like most things from that time in my life, I don't remember Stephania Allessio. But Mom always said she was my first friend. That we spent hours in each other's company. We shared a babysitter who called us Tweedledee and Tweedledum.

I thought about her often, more than you'd think someone could of a person she didn't remember the first thing
about. I wondered whether if we'd never moved, if Dad had
never died, maybe Stephania Allessio and I would have
grown up the best of friends. The kind who finish each
other's sentences. The type that makes people say, "Just look
at those two."

Because even though I made other friends, somehow I
always felt like a *one*. Singular. Alone.

A Dee without a Dum.

Aaron Finklestein.

Kindergarten. The Blue Room. We napped side by side.
His orange curls would sometimes spill over onto my mat.
He sucked his thumb. I sucked my index finger. We had so
much in common.

But by second grade, when a boy wasn't supposed to have
a girl as a best friend, I lost him to Gavin Bell.

Georgia McNulty.

My research partner on the Eiffel Tower. Fourth grade—
Ms. Sherman's class. We had to work on the project outside
of school, so she came to my house. This was before the
Cheese Shop when Mom worked from home trying to
launch a mail-order business selling holiday decorations.

We came home hungry and Mom served us éclairs and
used an embarrassing French accent, but Georgia McNulty
laughed and whispered *Your mom is so funny*, and later she
confided that she had a crush on our science teacher.

The project lasted a month or so during which Georgia

McNulty came over seven times. We built a replica of the Eiffel Tower out of paper clips and got an A, and then a few days later I heard that she'd told a bunch of people that my house was small and messy, both of which were true, but I stopped speaking to her anyway.

Alison Samuel.

Kids said Alison Samuel ate her own boogers, and I have no proof that this was true, but once you become known as the girl who eats her own boogers, it's a reputation that's hard to shake.

I felt sorry for Alison, which I now realize is not the greatest foundation upon which to build a friendship. We started sitting next to each other in fifth grade, when we were finally allowed to choose our own seats. Choice might be a generous way to put it considering nobody wanted to sit next to Alison Samuel, and nobody seemed all that interested in sitting next to me, which got me wondering what I was known as.

The girl who . . . ?

Alison hated school and she hated everyone in the school, and she hated the way our art teacher tucked her shirts into her skirts and the way our PE coach chewed his gum. All this started to rub off on me—hate has its way of doing that—so I spent most of fifth grade in a fairly miserable state.

Then her parents decided to send her to a private school where she could start over, though I have my doubts that even without a reputation for ingesting the contents of her nose, Alison Samuel was any happier.

Georgia McNulty.

Georgia returned to my life without apology, which was fine by me, because over the intervening years my decision to stop speaking to her struck me as rash.

As usual, Georgia was standing by her locker with Beatrice and Janice. It was just before lunchtime. I stopped to tie my shoes. My laces were new; rainbow ones I'd swapped out for the usual boring white ones, and intended for roller skates, they were way too long.

"Hey, Drew," she called. "Wanna come with us to Antonio's?"

I paused, waiting for her to add *Just kidding*, a favorite joke of the moment among the girls in sixth grade. But she just let the invitation hang there.

"Sure," I said.

So I walked with Georgia and her two best friends off campus to Antonio's for lunch, which those of us with permission from our parents were allowed to do, and I sat with them as they talked and laughed. Occasionally one of them would address a question or a comment to me and I'd say something back, and sometimes they'd say *Shut up*, which actually meant that what I'd said was interesting, and then sometimes they'd act as if I hadn't said anything at all.

The next two years continued in pretty much the same fashion.

They were my friends, but they weren't people I could ask about what was happening in the bathroom with Geraldine Moore and all those boys, and I certainly couldn't ask them about the things in Dad's Book of Lists.

Still, I was grateful to have a group of friends, though I never quite got over the suspicion that if I'd done a better double-knot that morning with my rainbow laces I might have spent sixth and seventh grades alone.

This summer I would get a taste of friendlessness.

They were all gone. Georgia and Beatrice and Janice were off to an eight-week program together on the campus of a boarding school near London. Georgia to study acting. Beatrice and Janice to study the same, because that's what Georgia was doing.

I didn't mind. I was relieved, even. In a way, they'd started leaving me behind before buying tickets to London. They had boyfriends. They hated their parents. They didn't get why I liked hanging out after school in a shop that stank like sweaty feet. Rats made them squeal.

Anyway, I still had Swoozie. I still had Nick. I still had Hum. And I thought I still had Mom.

mom, a vanishing act

The first sign should have been that coiled snake of calculator ribbon. Or maybe that Mom was doing less yoga, eating more cheese, and still losing weight.

I'd never bothered to think about the challenges of opening a new business. How stressful that might be. To me, the shop was all fun and adventure. It was a place to hang out.

I'd been dreaming all year of escaping school: the narrow hallways, the smell of lead and chalk, the crushing weight of my own invisibility. All I wanted was to be with Nick, to watch him work the new pasta machine. He'd promised to teach me to make squid ink linguini, which came out black and left your hands ash-gray for days.

That this new machine had cost the equivalent of several months' rent on the shop didn't matter to me. Nick loved it;

he became not just the guru of broken electronics, but also an artisan of the lightest, most delicate pastas. The way I saw it, the investment paid for itself.

But what did I know?

If I'd heard the words *recession* or *economic downturn* I didn't take them in. They were the sorts of things deep-voiced men on the radio droned on about when all I could think of was how to switch the dial back to KISS-FM. I didn't understand that those words struck terror in the heart of a small-business owner like my mother.

All I knew was that after the close call with the freezer and the Belcher the year before, things seemed to be going fine. We were about to start carrying desserts! It was shaping up to be a perfect summer.

On Monday, my first day of work, Mom had already left by the time I woke up. The shop didn't open until ten, and I'd always assumed that was when Mom went in, with her gigantic ring of keys, and opened the front door to a waiting customer or two.

On school days, the bus picked me up at 7:42. Mom waved goodbye from the window. And on weekends I'd sleep until eleven (this was a new phenomenon, my love of sleep), so on Saturdays it was no surprise to me that Mom was already gone by the time I got up. We were closed Sundays. Sunday was our day together.

On this morning, when I came downstairs at nine, there was a note on the table beside a hardened English muffin. It was timed in the top left corner—Mom always timed her notes to the minute.

7:51

Birdie—

off to the shop. come in whenever you like.
or don't come in at all. It's your first day of sum_
mer. You're free! Enjoy yourself! whatever you de_
cide, keep me in the loop.
Love you madly.

She always timed her notes and she always signed off
Love you madly, even when the notes weren't so cheery. Like
the kind that would appear on the top of a pile of dirty dishes.

3:27

Birdie—

Exactly whose job do you suppose it is to
wash these? Mine? I think not! Stop treating this
house like a hotel. Last time I checked we had no
cleaning staff.
Love you madly.

Why would she suggest I take this day off? It was my first
day. She needed me, didn't she? Nick needed me. Monday
was ravioli day. He'd make enough to sell fresh for the next
three days and then some more for the freezer.

I took a shower, then thought too much about my outfit.

I put on a brand-new pair of socks. From the list of Ways to Start the Day Off Right: *socks, fresh from the package.*

I got Hum settled into my bag and started to walk. It was a little over two miles. I could have ridden my bike, but I worried about what the helmet would do to my hair.

When I arrived Mom was on the phone. She waved and made a *Shoot me now* sign with her fingers and rolled her eyes back in her head, which I took to be all in fun, and didn't read as any sort of commentary about tough times on the business end of things.

I went over to the bulletin board and looked for my name on the time sheet. Not there. I turned to ask Mom, but she gave me the flat of her hand—the universal symbol for *Don't even think about interrupting this phone call.*

I grabbed an apron. I did a quick under-the-radar check inside my backpack to see that things were cool with Hum before hanging it up on the hook by the door and joining Nick at the pasta machine.

We kept it in the front window. People loved to stop and watch Nick make pasta. Mothers with their children clutching dripping ice cream cones. Women in sweat suits with small dogs straining at their leashes. Girls in Brownie uniforms, clustered together like a swarm of bees.

Nick had flour in his hair. "Hey, kiddo," he said.

God, how I hated when he called me kiddo.

He patted a stool and I climbed up.

"Hands?"

I showed him my clean hands. Front and back. He gave them a quick squeeze.

"Let's do this thing."

We were making pumpkin ravioli; I loved the sweet cinnamony smell of the filling. But first we needed something to hold that filling in.

I rolled up my sleeves. As the first yellow sheet of egg pasta emerged from the machine—it always reminded me of my much-loved Play-Doh factory—Nick cut it and laid it across the twelve-inch span I made with my forearms. If I could look down and see the shape of my feet, we knew it was too thin.

"Perfection," I said.

I didn't just mean the pasta, but this day. The days that would follow. This was it. This was what I'd been waiting for: a summer in the company of Nick. Someplace I could be useful. Who else would check the thickness of the ravioli if not me?

The morning went as expected. Mom never did get off the phone. Swoozie manned the counter. I got to scoop the pumpkin filling into the little squares. Nick sealed them shut with the tines of a fork.

And then his lunch break came.

She was waiting for him out front, wearing a tank top and peasant skirt, right where strangers stopped to watch him work the pasta machine. Maybe that was how they met. Maybe she watched him from that window for weeks, months even, before gaining the courage to come in and ask him how long to boil angel hair.

He'd have told her that its proper name is capellini.

They'd have shared a smile.

Today he grabbed a baguette and a triangle of Brie. He took the remains of a jar of fig jam we were offering as a sample. He stuffed them in his messenger bag, threw it over his shoulder, and walked out the front door with its maddening jingle, right into her bare arms. She climbed onto the back of his Vespa and wrapped those arms around his waist, and they disappeared. He was allowed thirty minutes for lunch.

He took thirty-three.

I used all of those minutes to give myself a pep talk. *Nick has a girlfriend. Of course Nick has a girlfriend. How could he not have a girlfriend?* I sat in the freezer in a too-big parka, trying to hold myself together.

That was where Swoozie found me. Talking to myself, which I was able to pass off as talking to Hum, which struck me as slightly less pathetic.

She put her arm around me.

"You know, Birdie, this isn't something you should worry yourself over."

"I'm not worried."

"This is grown-up stuff. And you're"—she reached over and stroked my frozen cheek—"still a child."

Swoozie had never talked down to me like this before, and it stung more than the cold.

"I'd like to be alone."

Still, she sat.

"So unless there's something you need in here . . ." These were the most unkind words I could find with which to strike back.

"You sure?"

"Positive."

She left, and it wasn't until I came out again to find Mom still sitting at her desk, writing checks, that it occurred to me that maybe Swoozie wasn't talking about Nick and his new girlfriend.

Maybe she was talking about Mom and the business.

sunday

I knew it wasn't fair to blame Nick for my disastrous first day on the job, but that didn't stop me from sulking all week and leaving Nick stranded, alone with his machine and his sidewalk admirers.

I took up a post behind the cheese counter. I kept the case stocked and the sample plate full. I cut, wrapped, and weighed cheeses, and for those who sought my advice, I gave it. Most people gravitated to Swoozie, whose size and age gave a stronger impression of a long and close relationship with cheese. But for those willing to take the chance on a sulky girl who must have worn her dashed dreams of summer all over her pale face, I had good advice to give. I knew my cheeses.

I also emptied the trash. I wiped down the countertops. I kept the cash register filled with bills and coins for change even though I wasn't permitted to operate the register myself. And I performed my favorite task—taking the bread we didn't sell that day, the fresh pasta it was too late to freeze, and whatever cheeses were past their prime out to the alley behind the shop. Come morning, without fail, the piles had always disappeared.

All week long I had wondered why I wasn't on the sign-in sheet where Mom tracked the hours of her employees. I waited until Sunday, our day off, to broach the subject.

We went to our favorite spot for breakfast: Bartholomew's. It had become a tradition, although with my new devotion to sleep these Sunday breakfasts had turned into something more like Sunday brunches.

She ordered a latte. She always let me have a sip or two, but this time I asked if I could have my own.

"No, Birdie. Not yet."

"Why?"

"Caffeine stunts your growth, and I'm pretty sure you've got some growing left to do."

I hoped not. I was already taller than most of the boys in my class, and I imagined this was the reason none of them seemed remotely interested in me. Although I couldn't really blame my height for the total lack of interest I had in them. It was a two-way street. I was too tall. They were too immature. Too un-Nicklike to warrant my attention.

"Fine." I said. I began to build a tower out of the coffee creamers.

Mom sat back and closed her eyes to the sun. We'd scored one of Bartholomew's primo tables out on the deck. She was a burner, and she'd burn herself to peeling. She loved the sun with unwavering devotion.

"How come I'm not on the time sheet?" I asked.

"What?"

"The time sheet at the shop. My name's not on it."

She opened her eyes. Puzzled. "So?"

"So, I work there too, you know."

"Okay. I'll put your name on the sheet. Why are you being so pissy?"

In the ten months or so we'd been in business I'd come to the shop most days after school, and a fair amount of Saturdays too. I'd never been paid for any of my time, but now this was a job. My job. My summer. And there were things I wanted to buy.

I wanted a new leather jacket. Shawls were so over. Georgia and Beatrice and Janice had leather jackets. So did Geraldine Moore. I didn't want to be like the rest of the girls at school, and yet I wanted that jacket.

I'd convinced myself that I'd gotten there first. That I'd imagined this jacket, pictured myself wearing it, before everyone else had raced out and bought one.

So that's why I was being pissy.

"Am I going to get paid for my work or not?"

"Birdie. You're thirteen years old."

"I'm aware of that, Mom. Thanks."

She looked at me. I knew she was counting to five. That's what she did when she started to get angry or tense, when she worried she might say something she didn't want to say. She always encouraged me to do the same. I rarely made it past one.

"Listen, Drew. It's not that I don't value you or the time you give to the shop. I do. You're part of the team. And I love that you love to pitch in. But you're only thirteen.

There are child labor laws. I can't just put you on my payroll. And even if I could, I can't afford to pay you anyway. We're barely squeaking by as it is."

The waitress had delivered my eggs, and I broke the yolks with my fork. I watched the bright yellow spill to the edges of my plate.

"This shop is ours, Birdie. Yours and mine. It's our future. You don't see my name on that time sheet, do you? That's because it's my shop, so I'm not really an employee. And neither are you."

She reached for my hand. I could feel myself forgiving her. The unclenching of some interior muscles too remote to know by name.

"So." She leaned forward in her seat. "What do you think of her?"

"Who?"

"You know."

Of course I knew, but that didn't mean I had to cop to it. I shrugged.

"Nick's new girlfriend?" She asked. "The blonde? Little Miss Perfect?"

"Oh, her." What was Mom doing? Was she trying to rub it in? "I didn't really get a chance to meet her."

"She's sweet. Really sweet. I just hope she doesn't go and get her heart broken."

"Yeah. Poor her."

"Oh, Birdie," Mom said. "I know you adore Nick. So do I. He's adorable. But he isn't worthy of your heart. Save that for someone your age, for someone who's able to truly accept it, because it's the most beautiful heart I know."

She reached across the table and placed her hand where she thought my heart must be, though I knew from biology class she was a little too far to the left.

I'd suffered through Mom's speeches about hearts before. She had visited the land of heartbreak, and it was the fact that I was pretty sure she still dwelled there, or at least dropped by frequently, that made these sorts of conversations unbearable. Because no matter how hard it was to sit across from my mother and talk about what I might be feeling, it was loads harder to see my mom as someone who knew this sort of exquisite pain too.

So I did what I always did in these situations.

I changed the subject.

"What are we seeing later?"

On Sundays we went to the movies. We saw everything. Mom didn't care if I saw movies with R ratings, and that gave me the rare glint of cool when I'd talk about them Monday at school.

She winced. "Not today, I'm afraid."

"What? Why?"

"It's work, honey. I've got to go into work. Remember"—she reached over and pushed my hair off my forehead—"this is our future."

I had no reason to think she wasn't telling me the truth. What else but work could possibly keep her from honoring our Sundays at the movies? It was our tradition.

From Dad's Book of Lists—Traditions: *a swim in the ocean on the summer solstice, a cigar on New Year's Day, singing my Birdie to sleep.*

From my list of traditions: *Sundays at the movies with Mom.*

on the loose

It wasn't until after seven that I noticed Hum was missing. I know that doesn't exactly make me the poster girl for the proper care and feeding of rats, but there you have it. Hum was gone.

It was Wednesday. I'd been in the shop for the better part of the day, though I was starting to come in later and later. I wasn't getting paid. Nick had gone and fallen in love behind my back. Neither fact inspired in me a desire to get up early.

I left the shop at six p.m., closing time. I delivered the bread and the food we couldn't sell the next day to the alley and rode my bike home. Mom told me she had to stay late and she sent me home with some spinach farfalle and meat sauce to heat up. She didn't mind me riding my bike while it was still light out.

I knew I'd opened up my backpack before hopping on my bike to put the farfalle in, but I couldn't say whether I'd noticed if Hum was in his cage or not. All I knew was that now, shortly after seven, while I was just settling down to watch TV, I'd gone to get Hum out of my bag and found him gone. Missing.

The first thing I did was start calling his name, which was ridiculous. He was a rat, not a dog. He didn't come when called.

I searched the entire house. I returned to my backpack, panic rising in me. It was then that I noticed a chewed-through hole in the bottom right corner.

The last time I'd seen Hum? When I arrived at work, sometime after noon. I sneaked a look at him, as I always did, before hanging my bag on the hook near the back door. My crime was not checking on him at closing time.

I did another thorough search of the house. It was a small house, as Georgia McNulty had so kindly told everyone, so it didn't take long. No Hum.

This presented a terrible problem. If he wasn't here, he was in the shop. And Mom was in the shop, working late. I couldn't very well call her up and ask her to look around for my rat.

I would have called Swoozie, but she had left when I did. She'd offered me a ride in her beat-up old Porsche, a car that might have given her some edge except that the tiny back was so filled up with her crap there wasn't even room for my bike.

I'd have considered swallowing my pride and calling Nick, but Nick never stayed past closing, even in his pre-girlfriend days.

I had no choice. I had to get on my bike and ride back to the shop in what was left of the daylight. I had to search inside and out, high and low, and I had to do all this without Mom noticing me. After all, he was my Hum, His Excellency the Lord High Rat Humboldt Fog. I couldn't imagine a world without him.

I dressed all in black. This was what I'd seen people do in the movies—cat burglars, creepers, those who did not want to be seen. I grabbed my ugly orange vest with reflector strips for the ride back home.

When I arrived at the shop it was dark. Nobody there.

I peered in the front window. Nick's pasta corner was closed up, his stool on the counter, the floors swept clean of semolina. The only lights were the small red power lights signaling that the refrigerated cases were running. I could see through the shop to the edge of Mom's office, and her chair, pushed away from her desk, sitting empty. There didn't seem to be any light coming from the rear of the store, but I crept around to the alley to have a look, just to be sure.

I could peer through the back windows without standing on my tiptoes, something I couldn't do when the shop first opened.

Total darkness.

I was baffled but also relieved. I had a key. I could look for Hum without any sneaking and creeping. The shop was mine to search. But where was Mom?

Then I heard it. A noise behind me. Behind the Dumpster to my left. I stopped breathing. I closed my eyes. I didn't move, but I listened.

Whispering. Someone was back there. Behind the Dumpster. Whispering to somebody else.

I thought: *Isn't this how tragic stories end? With a girl in a*

Dumpster? A girl who had gone out on her own, too late into the night? A girl someplace she shouldn't be? Nobody could explain why she was in that alley. Why she'd left the safety of her own home. She was a good girl. A careful girl. And now she'd gone and wound up in a Dumpster.

I weighed my options. Running around front for my bike would bring me too close to the Dumpster and the whispering. Better to leave my bike and run like crazy in the opposite direction. I was fast. My already-long legs were getting longer, or else I wouldn't have been able to see in this back window without standing on my toes.

But I didn't move. I was frozen in place, with my face pressed against the glass.

More whispering. Some shushing. *Shhh-shhh-shhh.*

And then a clicking, followed by a high-pitched squeaking that I knew well. The sound Hum made when he was happy.

"Hum?" I whispered. It didn't matter that he didn't know his name, that he never responded to it; I couldn't think of what else to do. "Hum?" I said louder.

I didn't want to go behind the Dumpster. I wanted my rat to come to me. I wanted him to break free from his captor, and I wanted to grab him, and lock him in his cage, and hop on my bike and race home.

I heard some shuffling. The rustling of paper. And then a voice.

"Hello?"

It was a kind voice. The voice of a boy.

"Hello?" I responded.

"Um, if you're trying to hum, the idea is to close your

mouth and sing through your lips. You don't actually say *hum*."

I had to admit, now that it was pointed out to me, calling out the word *hum* might sound strange to the uninformed ear.

"I know how to hum," I said. "I'm just calling my rat. That's his name."

The boy stepped out from behind the Dumpster. He had a tangle of black curls, holes in the knees of his jeans, a cut on his cheek, and my rat on his shoulder.

"You mean him?" He lifted his hand to the waiting rat's mouth and fed him a small scrap of something orange.

"Yes. That's Hum. My rat."

"And who are you?"

I should have asked this question first. *He* was the one hiding behind the Dumpster behind *my* shop. *He* was the one holding *my* rat and feeding him God knows what. *Who are you?* I should have asked, shouted even, but instead I just said, "I'm Drew."

"Well, then why does everyone call you Birdie?"

"I'm sorry. Do I *know* you?"

"I'm Emmett," he said, and he stuck out his hand, and as I took it, Hum crawled down his arm and ran up the length of mine. "Emmett Crane."

emmett crane

It was obvious why I was there in that alley calling out the word *Hum*.

Emmett Crane's story proved harder to unravel.

It turned out he knew I was the daughter of the woman who owned the store. Understandably, he was just confused about my name.

I explained that my mother called me Birdie because my name used to be Robin. This required mentioning my dead father, to which he responded, "Oh. So I guess that wasn't your father in the Honda?"

"What Honda?"

"Or maybe it was a Toyota. I'm not particularly interested in cars."

"What car?" I was getting agitated.

"The silver Honda or maybe Toyota that came to pick up your mother after you left on your bike."

I couldn't think of one single person we knew who drove a silver car.

I sat down on the rickety bench we kept in the alley, where Swoozie would come to *get some fresh air*, which really meant *smoke a cigarette*.

He sat down next to me. He smelled both sweet and sharp, like something I knew but couldn't quite place.

"I'm sorry," he said. "Did I say something I shouldn't have?"

"No." I took Hum off my shoulder and held him in my lap. "It's just . . . she's supposed to be here. Working late."

"Well, adults can't always be counted on to do what they say they're going to do." He picked at the hole in the knee of his jeans. "At least not in my experience."

Already I was having a longer conversation with this boy than I'd had with any boy my age since the days of Aaron Finklestein. I was guessing he was my age, or maybe a little bit older.

"How'd you get that cut on your cheek?" I asked. "It wasn't . . ." I looked down at Hum in my lap.

"No, no, of course not." He reached up to his face. "This is nothing. Just me being clumsy. Your rat"—he reached over and tickled Hum under his chin—"is a gentle soul."

I couldn't stop stroking Hum's head. Only an hour or so had passed between when I noticed him gone and finding him in this alley, but that was enough to make me particularly appreciate the feel of his fur between my fingers.

Emmett held out another orange scrap and Hum took it greedily.

"Tell me that's not cheese," I said.

"I could tell you that, but then I'd be lying."

"Please don't feed him cheese. I know everyone thinks that's what rats eat, but cheese is bad for rats."

"It's not bad for *your* rat."

"How do you figure that?"

"Well, cheese is bad for some rats, just like cheese is bad for some people. But he tolerates it fine. See?" He fed him another piece. This time I noticed a green fleck in the orange, which I recognized as coming from the wedge of Cotswold I'd left in the alley at closing.

"Just because he's eating it doesn't mean it's good for him," I said.

"Yes it does. Rats are careful about what they eat. I know they get a bad rap for eating everything, you know, like Templeton in *Charlotte's Web?*"

Of course I knew; it was my favorite book. And I'd seen the movie more times than I could count.

"But actually," he continued, "they won't eat anything that makes them sick. They'll try a bite, give it time, and if they feel fine they'll eat more. I gave Hum his first bit of cheese an hour ago." He handed him another piece. "And he keeps coming back for more."

"How do you know all this?" I asked.

"Just because I don't know anything about cars doesn't mean I don't know anything about rats."

We sat in silence for a while, something I wasn't able to do with my friends who were girls. I had no idea if he knew what he was talking about, but I knew I liked hearing him talk.

It was getting dark. I needed to get home so I could beat Mom back. She'd return to collect her car, and she hadn't done that yet, so I had at least a little bit of time left. I didn't feel much like leaving, but I stood up and started to lure Hum back into his cage.

"So, what are you doing hanging around back here, anyway?" It should have been the first thing I asked him.

He looked at me like I'd said "What color is the sky?" or "What is two plus two?"

"The food," he said. "It's delicious."

He walked me to my bike in front of the shop and watched as I put on my reflector vest.

"You can never be too careful." He smiled at me. "It's a dangerous world out there."

"See you around," I said as I rode away.

"Yeah, see you around, Robin," he called.

the tin man

"His body was all done living."

That's what Mom used to say. It must have been something she read in a book. Or something a psychologist told her to tell a young child who sought some explanation for the sudden disappearance of her father. When I pushed Mom for more information about what part of his body was *all done living*, she told me it was his heart. It just stopped working.

I don't know what book or psychologist told her it was a good idea to tell a young child that her father's heart stopped working, because I used to think that if only I'd given his heart more reason to work, it would never have gone and shut down.

But it did.

He was dead.

And I was too young to miss him. Or at least to remember missing him. I told myself as I grew up that I was lucky. I had my mother to myself. I didn't have to share her with anyone else. *Those poor kids*, I'd think. *How do they get by, how do they even hear themselves think, with all those other people in the house?*

My mother kept a picture of him on her dresser. His red hair mussed from sleep, holding his bundled baby with her dull brown hair on his bare chest. Their bedside lamp didn't give off enough light to show him clearly, but he looked peaceful. Happy. His heart full of reasons to keep beating.

When I thought of him, which wasn't often, I didn't think of that picture. I thought instead of the Tin Man from *The Wizard of Oz*. A creaky shell of a man with no heart at all.

But then I found his Book of Lists, and he slowly came to life again.

Careers I Never Want to Attempt: *coal miner, executioner, proctologist.* (I had to look that last one up, and it wasn't pretty.)

Pet Peeves: *people who have pet peeves.*

Greatest Loves: *my electric blue Schwinn Cruiser, my cream-colored Fender Telecaster, my Lizzie Aberdeen Solo, and our little Birdie.*

Two things occurred to me, studying these lists.

One: Life is short. I'd done my fair share of thinking about life span and how Dad, dead at thirty-three, helped keep down the average. But I hadn't stopped and thought about Hum, had never even wondered about the life span of a rat, which I came to learn averaged two years. So if my rat was lucky enough to be average, he was already halfway to his grave.

Two: Someone who keeps a list of all of these facts about himself is probably keeping it for a reason, so that someone can know him when he's no longer there. Dad must have been aware that his heart would stop beating, that his body would soon be *all done living,* or else why keep the list in the first place?

word games

I didn't see Emmett again for days, though it wasn't for lack of looking. I took the trash out hourly, causing Swoozie to glare at me like she'd just tasted a cheese of questionable freshness.

"The trash? Again?" She leaned in close. "Girl, you better not be smoking cigarettes on my bench out there or Lord help me, I will put you over my knee."

"No, Swoozie. It's nothing like that. I'm just trying to stay busy."

This wasn't entirely untrue. Business was slow. I was still boycotting Nick. He continued to make his spinach linguini and tomato spaghetti and saffron fettuccini without my help. Occasionally he'd shoot me a look, something like an exaggerated pout, but I'd turn the other way. It wasn't the worst thing, I figured, letting him miss me a little.

My frequent visits to the Dumpster produced nothing other than a spectacular waste of perfectly good garbage bags.

Emmett wasn't hanging out in the alley, he wasn't waiting for food, and he certainly wasn't waiting for me. Yet everything we left out back at closing disappeared by morning, so I guessed he still came by the shop after hours.

Since I'd patched the hole in my backpack and rewired the latch on Hum's cage, I had no reason to return to the alley at dusk. Even if I could have manufactured a reason, there was the problem of Mom, and sneaking out of the house unnoticed, because for the next several days after my visit to the alley, Mom came home and stayed.

I still had no answer to the mystery of the silver car. When she walked into our kitchen late the night I met Emmett, I took the casual approach. I knew from my own experience, and from the habits of my rat, that nobody likes to be backed into a corner.

"How was work?" I asked.

"You know," she answered. "Work is work."

"You were at the shop?"

"Where else would I be?"

"That's what I'm asking you."

At this point Mom walked over to where I was sitting with my legs dangling off the counter and she pulled me to her, kissing the top of my head.

"I'm knackered," she said. She put both hands on my cheeks. "Too tired for word games, Birdie. I'm turning in."

She left the room and I sat there, my heart racing. My cheeks, right where she'd touched me, burning. *She's lying.*

I replayed our conversation in my head and realized, as I took it apart piece by piece, that actually, she hadn't lied at all. That she was, and maybe always had been, the master of word games.

Work is work. Where else would I be? A game of words.

This too: *His body was all done living.*

I didn't follow her up the stairs of our tiny house and pound on her door, demanding an explanation. I was pretty sure that was the job of a mother, not a daughter. I decided instead to file this incident away. That I might need it later. That there might come a time when I would want to show her how she hadn't always been honest with me. How everyone is capable of lies or mistakes or untruths or even clever games. I wasn't exactly planning or plotting anything, I was merely filing.

And I was collecting. A small piece of a puzzle.

That night I went up to bed in a silent house, safe in my role of the girl who doesn't break the rules, who doesn't upset the natural order and demand explanations from the adults around her. I slept late and then I went to work. I took out the trash, and I did this over and over again until finally, on Monday, when I went out to the Dumpster with my first garbage bag of the day, I found his note.

I might have discarded it like another piece of trash if he hadn't thought to turn the scrap of paper into something eye-catching.

It was on Swoozie's bench, facing me just as I came out the back door. The same spot where I'd held Hum and Emmett had fed him Cotswold, where we had talked about silver cars.

It was a paper bird that I didn't recognize right away as a crane.

59

His namesake.

I unfolded it carefully, with the uncomfortable feeling of destroying a work of art. I wouldn't have taken it apart at all if I hadn't noticed my initials written on its tail.

DRS

The crane slowly turned into a square of paper, revealing this note, in tiny, perfect writing.

Dear Robin—
    I hope that vest got you home safely and that Hum has been a good boy. I'm guessing he has, since I haven't seen you in your burglar costume lately. If you don't have to work tomorrow, meet me at Garfield Park at noon.
P.S. What's the cheese with the red marble in it? Weird but tasty.

a day off

It was port wine cheddar, and it wasn't for everyone, but I adored it. Truth be told, it could have spent another day in the case, but I'd taken it out to the alley wondering if Emmett might like it too.

I called the shop in the morning to tell Mom I wouldn't be coming in, which felt easier than telling her the news to her face. She might have asked me what my plans for the day involved, and I wasn't as good a liar as she was.

Nick answered the phone.

"The Cheese Shop."

"Lizzie Solo, please."

"Drew?"

"Yes."

"It's Nick."

Of course I knew it was Nick. "Hi."

"Where are you, kiddo? I'm feeling some squid ink coming on."

"I'm not going to make it in today."

"You okay?"

"Yeah."

A pause. "Are *we* okay?"

A wave of warmth for Nick washed over me. His crooked smile. His sea-green eyes. His messy blond hair. I'd tried being angry with him, tried hating him for loving the girl in the peasant skirt, but I could feel now that it wasn't sticking.

I had to give myself credit. Any girl could admire a boy like Nick—crooked, sea-green, messy Nick—but in the end what I liked best about him was his kindness. He was, always, so very kind to me.

"Of course we're okay," I said.

"Good. Because work is boring without you. And my ravioli is chewy."

"I'll be back tomorrow. Tell Mom I need a day off, will you?"

"Will do."

"Thanks."

"And Drew?"

"Yeah?"

"Enjoy your day off. Paint your toenails. Or eat a banana split. Do something for *yourself*. Something that's not about your mom, or the shop. Something just for you."

We hung up and I stared at the phone for a good minute or two. I wanted to pick it up again. To call someone and talk. To read aloud the note from the paper crane and then read it again. To ask what I should wear. Hair up or down? I didn't have that person in my life. I might have called Georgia, but we didn't have an international calling plan, and even if she'd still been in town, I might not have called her anyway.

I needed someone. At the very least, I needed someone to tell me where to find Garfield Park.

I'd lived here all my life. Maybe when I was a baby I had graced Garfield Park with my drooly presence, but now I couldn't figure out for the life of me where to find the place. The only parks I knew of were the ones where I used to play soccer, and I'd given up the sport years ago.

We kept a map of the state of California in the car, but Mom had the car. Anyway, our town barely made the map— we weren't Los Angeles, we weren't San Francisco, we were merely a dot in between.

I put Hum in my bag, hopped on my bike, and rode over to see the one person I knew who knew everything. Well, maybe not everything. I wouldn't have asked her about Geraldine Moore, for example, but when it came to finding out anything about this town, that person was Mrs. Mutchnick.

If I thought things were slow at our place, then they were dead, gone, packed in ice at Mrs. Mutchnick's fabric store. I entered through the back door, hoping my visit would go unnoticed by anyone staring out the window from Mom's shop across the street.

P&L Fabrics felt like a different universe from the Cheese Shop. Everything was heavy, dark, covered in dust. The old wood floors creaked. The sink in the bathroom dripped. Clearly, a store selling fabric wasn't held to the same standards as one selling food.

Mrs. Mutchnick stood when she saw me and rubbed her hands together like an excited child.

"Ooooh. Let me see him. Give him here."

I unzipped my bag and took out Hum's cage. He made his happy clicking sound. I had a feeling Hum knew Mrs. Mutchnick, knew she was the one responsible for delivering him to his new life with me, for rescuing him from his fate as a boa constrictor's lunch.

He leapt into her outstretched hands.

It was summer, the days of endless light, but her store felt like a place you'd settle in for a long winter's nap. I'd never seen a customer at P&L Fabrics, but I wasn't sure Mrs. Mutchnick cared too much about actual sales. She'd bought the building and opened the store with her husband, the L of P&L, over forty years earlier. He'd been dead for the last ten of those years, and the shop gave her someplace to go.

"To what do I owe the pleasure of your company?" she asked.

"Hum missed you. He's always begging me to bring him by for a visit."

"He's a prince, our Humboldt Fog." She scratched him between the ears.

She asked me about the cheese business. She'd heard most of the Euclid Avenue merchants were having a rough time of it, though the diner was going like gangbusters. When times are tough, people turn to comfort: a cup of tomato soup, blueberry pancakes, a chocolate malted.

"Things seem okay to me," I said. "Maybe a little slow."

I made a note to myself: *We should start making the ultimate comfort food: macaroni and cheese.*

"Do you know Garfield Park?" I asked.

"Of course I do. I used to take picnics there with Mr. Mutchnick. A lifetime ago. It's lovely."

"Could you tell—"

"It's named after James Garfield, of course. Our twentieth president. He was shot by a disgruntled lawyer, as if there's any other type of lawyer. Do you know about Garfield, or did you assume the park was named for that asinine orange cat? Sometimes I wonder about your generation. If you're getting any education at all."

It was a challenge, keeping Mrs. Mutchnick on point, and she seemed not to know or care whether anyone was remotely interested in what she was saying. This might have had something to do with why nobody seemed to shop there.

"Mrs. Mutchnick—" I reached over and put my hand on her forearm. "Can you tell me where Garfield Park is? I'm meeting a friend and I'm already late."

"Yes, dear. But it's a hike. You have to go to where Capri Drive dead-ends and there's a trail you can catch through the brush. I've been after the fire marshal forever about it. It's a hazard, all that dry brush. Anyway, the trail will lead you to the park. It's a good half-mile straight uphill, but well worth it. The views are to die for. Are you picnicking?"

I nodded. I'd gone to collect food for Hum and then decided it wouldn't hurt to bring along some cheese and bread and what was left of the fruit tart Mom had baked last night.

Mrs. Mutchnick returned Hum and walked over to the corner, where bolts of fabric were stacked on top of each other like a gigantic pile of pickup sticks. She pulled one out from the bottom, grabbed a pair of shears, cut a large square, and then folded it up.

"Here. For your picnic. Something to sit on."

"Really?"

"Yes, of course. I've got more material here than I know what to do with."

I slipped it into my backpack. I paused before speaking again, hesitant to start up a whole new conversation. "Mrs. Mutchnick, do you ever think of leaving what you don't need out back behind the store?"

"No, I can't say I ever thought of that."

"It's just that someone who really needs it might come along and take it."

She squeezed my hand with affection. "It's a wonderful idea, Drew. Now get out of here. Don't keep your friend waiting. Time is precious."

garfield park

As I walked up the hill I found myself thinking of one of the items on Dad's list of Things I'd Like to Do but Probably Never Will: *climb Mount Kilimanjaro*.

My dead father and I were different. I had no desire to climb Mount Kilimanjaro.

Mom was always after me to get out and *do* something. To stay, as she liked to call it, heart-healthy. I rode my bike most places, but that was all. I much preferred to read about Belgian cheeses while sitting behind the counter in a quiet store. And no, I did not want to accompany Mom to one of her yoga classes. It wasn't that I was getting plump or even curvy—I was still growing in only one direction: up. But as I climbed this mountain my breathing grew heavy and my shirt stuck to my back with sweat, and I started to wonder, grudgingly, whether Mom might have a point.

Maybe if my dad hadn't died we'd have gone hiking together. Maybe it would have been something we did on

Saturdays, just the two of us. We'd lose ourselves in the wild and talk about life. We'd wear hats. Sunglasses. We'd carry special matching packs. Maybe I'd be in better shape, and this walk wouldn't be taking such a toll on me.

It hadn't occurred to me to bring water. It was hot and I was thirsty. Dad would never have let me forget water.

I started to have a crisis of faith.

What am I doing? Who is this Emmett Crane? What if this is all a big joke and there's nobody waiting at this park?

I plodded along until I reached a fork in the path. Not a metaphorical fork but an actual fork, and I cursed Mrs. Mutchnick, who rarely spared a detail yet had somehow managed to forget to tell me whether to bear right or left.

And then I saw it.

A paper crane. In the brush in front of me. I unfolded it.

> keep right. You're almost there.
> Did you bring anything to eat?
> I don't know about you, but I'm starving.

I put it in my back pocket, continued on, and then paused before reaching the crest of the hill to catch my breath and wipe my forehead with the hem of my tank top.

I took the final steps, and there he was, in the middle of a field of green—an oasis amid so much dried-out earth. I wasn't a worrier particularly, but Mrs. Mutchnick's fire concerns had followed me up that hill. Fires were common in this part of California, especially in summer, especially in the hills. A fire would devour this brush and me in a heartbeat.

But from this patch of green at the top of the dried-out hill you could see the ocean, endless and blue. The world, my world, felt full of possibility.

He was stretched out on his back, his eyes closed, and he'd rolled up the cuffs of his jeans with the holes in the knees. Beside him sat a large bottle of water. I walked toward him until my shadow fell over him. He sat up and peered at me from under the palm of his hand.

He held out the bottle.

"You look thirsty."

I put my backpack down and unzipped it. "And you look hungry."

He reached inside, but instead of grabbing for the cheese or the bread or the tart he went for Hum's cage. He mimicked Hum's happy clicking sound so perfectly, I thought it came from Hum himself.

"Hey, boy," he whispered between clicks. "Good boy."

Emmett was the only person other than Mrs. Mutchnick who genuinely loved my rat. Mom had finally come around to accepting that he was a part of our lives, so long as he didn't get too close. Swoozie and Nick tolerated him; they'd even scratch his belly or head when prodded. Georgia, Beatrice, and Janice shrank back in horror at the sight of him, making it clear that he was not welcome in our circle, lest they become known as friends of the Rat Girl.

But Emmett. He had a way with Hum.

I took the fabric Mrs. Mutchnick had given me and spread it out on the grass along with the food. All in all it didn't look like much of a picnic.

"That's Emmentaler." I pointed to the wedge I'd brought. "Which is really just a fancy way of saying Swiss cheese. Some pear and cranberry tart. And day-old French bread."

"Day-old bread gets a bad rap," he said, tearing off a hunk. "I love it. The fresh-baked stuff is way too soft."

He moved onto the blanket. I sat down next to him, and for a few minutes we just ate and stared out at the ocean. I was able, finally, to place his smell. He smelled like onions, but not like when Mom chopped them in the kitchen until my eyes watered, or like the ones frying on the griddle at Daisy's diner. He smelled like sweet, fresh onion. A pleasant sort of smell.

Sitting with him wasn't like sitting with Georgia and her crew with their never-ending talk. Nobody rushed to fill the silence.

"I don't think I've seen you around school," I said, finally.

I hoped this line would lead to more information. He might tell me what grade he was in, and then I could figure out his age. I was pretty sure he didn't go to my school—there wasn't a boy two grades above or below us who Georgia, Beatrice, and Janice hadn't dissected down to his brand of socks. If I learned where he went, I'd know volumes.

If he wasn't at Benjamin Franklin with me, then there was the private school, the only one in the area, where you got to call your teachers by their first names and choose your own reading for English. Why someone who had the money to go there would take day-old bread and cheese on its last legs from an alleyway was a mystery to me, but everything about Emmett was a mystery.

Finally, if he didn't go to Benjamin Franklin or the

private school, there was a vocational school for troubled kids where you went to learn service-industry skills or how to work farm equipment. I'd always suspected this school was made up, invented by parents as a threat for kids who weren't applying themselves academically. Sort of like threatening to call Santa's elves to report bad behavior.

"I'm new to the area," he said. "I moved here from down south a while back."

"Down south like Alabama?" We'd studied the Montgomery bus boycott in history that year, and it had entered my consciousness in a way I couldn't shake.

He laughed. "Down south like Los Angeles."

L.A. I'd never been, but I knew from movies and TV shows that everything, all those mansions and palm trees and swimming pools, all of it, was always bathed in blinding white light. How could someone ever go from there to here?

"So where are you living?"

"For now we're staying with some friends of my dad's, but when he finds a job we'll get a place of our own. A bachelor pad, he likes to say."

I'd told him about my father when I explained my name to him in the alley, but he didn't offer information about an absent mother, so I guessed it was something he wasn't eager to talk about.

I picked a blade of grass at the root. My father had taught my mother to whistle on a blade of grass, and she'd passed the trick on to me. I couldn't pull it off just then, so I tossed it away.

"Why would you ever come here?"

I'd always felt like I lived at a stop somewhere on the road to where life really happened. You didn't come here; you left here.

Sure, there was Swoozie, who'd moved from Wisconsin, but by her own admission real cities were too much for her. I always pictured Swoozie's beat-up Porsche running out of gas on Highway One, getting a tow to the Mobil station on the corner of Euclid and Fourth. I could see her getting out of her car, taking a look around, and deciding there were worse places to start over.

"Well, like I said, we have friends with a spare room." He didn't say this rudely, but he said it with an emphasized period, signaling the end of this part of our conversation.

"I'm almost fourteen," I blurted out, and immediately felt stupid. For one thing, my birthday was in January, so I was thirteen and a half, and everyone knows that only someone insecure about her age rounds up to the next year.

Also, he hadn't asked. So he might have wondered why I'd blurted out this random fact about myself. It could have been worse. I could have said *My favorite color is magenta*. But I didn't care about his favorite color. I cared about how old he was.

"Well, happy almost-birthday."

"Thanks."

"You're welcome. And thanks for coming all the way up here." He paused. "You're cool, Robin."

Once Chris Tanner told Georgia she was *hot* while he walked by her in the hall at school. Georgia told us at lunch. And she told us again the next day, and the day after that, and the day after that.

I'd thought, *What's the big deal?*

But now I knew.

Emmett Crane said I was cool, and had Georgia and Beatrice and Janice not been half a world away, I'd have told them. Over and over and over.

"Thanks," I said.

"By the way," he added, "don't be in any hurry to turn fourteen. Believe me, it's not all it's cracked up to be."

From Dad's Book of Lists, third on the list of Things I Wish I'd Known When I Was a Teenager: *it gets easier.*

Sometimes Dad's brevity was crazy-making. Would it have killed him to write more? What gets easier? Riding a bike? Learning a foreign language? Understanding the opposite sex?

When I read this for the first time I found it totally perplexing. Then I moved on and forgot it. But now these words found their way back to me, right at the moment when words were so hard to come by.

"I think it's supposed to get easier," I said. "So maybe fifteen will be better?"

He shrugged. "I hope you're right."

We'd finished everything. Every last scrap of Emmentaler and bread and tart. I peered in my bag anyway, hoping for something to extend our picnic, and I spied a flash of red. Hawaii's favorite candy bar. I'd picked it up the day before at Fireside Liquor and forgotten all about it.

I held it out. "Good News?"

"Sure," he said. "Who couldn't use some Good News?"

absolutely, positively fine

That night when Mom came home from the shop she asked me about my day. I said it was *fine*. She said *fine* wasn't an answer. I said *Okay, my day was absolutely, positively fine.*

The only thing remarkable about our exchange was that it was one of the first of this nature we'd ever had. I usually told Mom whatever she wanted to know. I didn't have anything to hide from her, and I assumed she had nothing to hide from me. We told each other everything. We were alone, together. Or together, alone. Us against the world. That sort of crap.

But now I lived in a universe of silver cars and books of lists and boys who appeared in alleys at dusk. Hidden parks on hilltops. Girls in peasant skirts.

Everything was changing.

"Let's try this again," she said slowly as she unpacked a bag of groceries. Along with some ravioli from the shop, she had vegetables for a salad and a bottle of wine for herself. "What did you do today? Did you read a book? Watch old reruns of *The Twilight Zone?* Shave your legs? Alphabetize your music collection?"

"I hung out with a friend."

Her face lit up. I knew she worried that I didn't spend enough time with people my own age. She'd pushed me not to drop soccer. To try summer camp. Join a club at school. I'd always said no, and the more she pushed the more irritated I'd become. Nobody likes to be worried over, or even worse, pitied, by her own mother.

Her euphoric look turned curious. "But I thought Georgia was in London, along with those other two girls."

"They are."

"So this is a new friend?"

"Yes."

"Great. That's just great. What's her name?"

I hesitated. I could have said Sally, Susan. I could've said Emma, cutting it pretty close. But I didn't see any reason why my new friendship with Emmett was something I had to lie about. She might not be thrilled about my having hiked up a dried-out hillside during fire season, but I couldn't see why she'd object to my becoming friends with a boy.

"His name is Emmett."

Mom continued chopping vegetables without missing a beat.

"And how do you know this boy?"

"I met him at the shop. . . . He's a big fan of our cheese." I grabbed a peeler and went after the cucumbers. "He's new to the area and I was just showing him around."

"That's nice, Birdie," she said. "Really nice." We continued to fix dinner standing side by side. We ate, and then Mom went off to bed early like she did so often those days and I flipped through the channels on the TV.

I thought about Emmett. About how he'd said I was cool.

I was stretched out on the couch, not moving a muscle, and yet my heart began to get that elusive cardiovascular workout.

How could it be? I'd loved Nick for most of a year. I wasn't a dreamer, so I had never really believed that Nick would or could love me back, that we'd live happily ever after in a kingdom of fresh pastas and cheese, but how he made me feel when I was near to him was something new to me. I'd thought it was something singular. Something specific to Nick, who smelled of the sea. And yet, that same rush had overtaken me as I'd reached the top of that climb and seen Emmett sprawled out on that grass.

Was I really that fickle? Was it really that easy for me to fall under the spell of another boy?

Well, at least I wasn't like Georgia and Beatrice and Janice—I didn't see every boy at school as a potential boy-friend. I didn't cut out pictures of movie stars from magazines and tape them to my walls. I didn't write my name out next to the name of some crush to see how they might look to-gether at the top of a wedding invitation.

I was not boy crazy. Really, I wasn't. But I was lonely, I guess. Mrs. Mutchnick had been right about me.

a face to unlock doors

I went to sleep with both of Emmett's notes under my pillow. I'd tried to reshape them back into birds, but the best I could come up with was something resembling a snail. Had they been able to sprout wings again, I'd have kept them on my bedside table where I could look at them, his words hidden inside. But instead I flattened them, tried my best to smooth out their wrinkles, and placed them where I knew they'd be safe. I didn't want to share them with Mom or anybody else.

If what I was attempting by sleeping on Emmett's notes was to bring him closer to me, it failed. I went to work in the morning and took the trash out five times that day. No paper cranes. That evening I left a truffled sheep's milk and a Dutch Edam with caraway seeds. Both were gone the next day, but no sign of, or from, Emmett Crane.

Seven days went by.

A week during which I began to question what, if

anything, was real about him. A week when Mom stayed out late on two different nights. A week spent patching things up with Nick. A week of dodging Swoozie's questions about what was eating at me.

"You wear your heart on your face," Swoozie told me over a game of gin rummy. She came to the house to hang out with me on the first of the two nights that week that Mom was "working late." "And your face tells me something is amiss in Birdland."

"I'm just tired." I was growing. I was a teenager. Wasn't I supposed to be tired? Wasn't it my right?

In the middle of that week Fletcher Melcher stopped by the shop. I saw him through the window and shifted into panic mode, grabbing a sponge and frantically wiping an already spotless countertop.

"Belcher alert!" I shouted, but Nick and Swoozie ignored me.

He didn't stick his nose in the air for a whiff or check any temperatures. He'd come to drop off a list of the health department's updated codes. His visit lasted only a minute, but he greeted everyone warmly, as if he were a kindly small-town mayor and not the evil villain of Euclid Avenue.

I retreated to Nick's pasta corner.

"Don't trust the nice-guy routine," I said under my breath. "He must be plotting something."

But Nick wouldn't play, and as I watched the Belcher leave, I felt a little let down.

I sulked as Nick layered lasagnas. We'd cut back on fresh pastas because they weren't selling as quickly as Mom had hoped, so we made meals we could freeze. Things you could throw in the oven and have ready to serve in under an hour. Food for working families. At my suggestion we'd tried out a recipe for macaroni and cheese, and it was a hit.

"It's Becca's birthday," Nick told me. "And I have absolutely no idea what to get her."

I started beating the eggs for our next project—spinach pasta sheets we'd stuff with ricotta and basil. I pretended not to hear him.

"Drew," Nick said. "This is me, pleading with you. I need your help. I need the advice of a girl. Girls know what other girls want. You're a girl. And you have great taste. And you're smart. So help me out."

I was flattered to be seen this way by Nick. I didn't understand girls. Yes, I was one, but all I knew was what *I'd* want. *I'd* want that leather jacket. But more than that, I'd want my boyfriend to know it was what I wanted. I'd want to know that he knew me well enough to figure it out on his own.

"Do you have any ideas?" I asked.

"Only one, but it's stupid."

"Go ahead."

"Well, she hates that I don't wear a helmet. So I thought maybe I'd buy one for each of us, like, matching helmets. Then she could stop wearing the fugly one she took from her brother, and I'd sacrifice half the reason I love my Vespa and cover up when I ride. You know, to make her happy."

I sat next to him on the pasta stool and didn't say anything.

"See? I told you it was a stupid idea."

"Nick. That's the least stupid idea I've ever heard."

"Really?"

"Really."

He shot me a beautiful grin.

The more days that went by, the more I scolded myself for getting that fluttery feeling about Emmett on the couch that night. I'd let my guard down.

While she packed a bag with my dinner, Mom told me she had to stay late at work for the third time in eight days. I'd already taken out the last of the day's trash and the extra cheese and bread. The front doors were locked. Swoozie had left early for a doctor's appointment. Nick and Becca had ridden off in their his and hers helmets.

"What do you have left to do?" I asked, gesturing around the shop. It was immaculate. Counters cleaned, floors swept, cases closed.

"Birdie," she said with exasperation, like I was a toddler on my hundredth *why* question of the day. "I have a crazy amount of paperwork to do. Bills to pay. Ledgers to balance."

"You aren't going anywhere?"

"Just to my desk."

"You aren't going out in a silver car?"

This flew from my mouth before I stopped to think, and the minute it was out there in the space between us I wished I could pull it back in.

"Whatever do you mean?" she said carefully.

"Nothing."

"It didn't sound like nothing."

I leaned over and hugged her. This caught her off guard, and it took a beat before she wrapped her arms around me. I held on to her tighter than I had in a long time. I squeezed her, hoping that it might somehow undo the conversation I'd started, because I didn't want to know.

I wanted to believe she'd be at her desk tonight. Paying bills. Balancing ledgers. So I held her like I did when I was younger, when that was all it took for everything to be right in the world.

"It was nothing," I said again, and I took my dinner-in-a-bag and rode home on my bike.

I put the bag in the fridge and ate a bowl of cereal instead. I was too lazy to boil water and too sick of pasta to face whatever she'd given me. I changed into my pajamas while it was still light and I put some of Mom's music on the downstairs stereo. Nothing was on TV. I scanned the bookshelf for something to read. I wished that I could draw or paint or do something, anything, well enough that I could lose myself in it and forget everything else. I turned the music up louder, but not so loud that I didn't hear the knock at the door.

Other than the fear of fire and the larger fear of nuclear war that was always in the background, we were pretty carefree around my house. Mom didn't lecture me about safety. She trusted me, trusted the universe enough to let me stay home alone and ride my bike wherever I wanted and not have to account in detail for my time away from her. I could say I showed a friend around town, for example, without being given the third degree.

However, when home alone I was to keep the front door

locked. I was not to open it to anyone. Packages could wait for delivery until the next day or sit out on the doorstep. Nothing was for sale that I needed to buy. No petition required my signature.

Standing there listening to the second round of gentle knocking, I couldn't remember a single time anyone had come to the house while I was home alone. I'd never been put to the test until now.

Round three.

And then a whisper: "Robin?"

There was only one person who would say my name like that. I unlocked the door.

He stood under the porch light.

"Hi," he said. There was something apologetic in his posture. At least, that was how I decided to take it. He was sorry for disappearing from my life for a week.

"Hi."

He smiled and brushed his black hair out of his eyes.

"Do you want to come in?" I asked.

He wiped his feet on our doormat. He'd have won Mom over with that single gesture.

He looked around the living room, standing still as if waiting to hear whether anyone else was in the house.

"I'm alone," I said.

"I saw that your mom's still at the shop, so, you know, I figured I'd find you here by yourself."

She's at work, I thought. *Just like she said.*

He still didn't move. He was listening to the music, a record of Irish folk songs I had playing only because that's what was already on the stereo. Mom loved this record. I'd roll my eyes at her whenever she put it on. *Again, Mom?*

But here I was, listening to it. Having that music on was like having Mom at home. It was the sound of not being alone.

I wished I had something else playing. Something cooler. Something Georgia would have had on when a boy stopped by to see her. And I really, really, *really* wished I hadn't already put on my pajamas. Flannel, old-man style, with pictures of sheep jumping over clouds.

"Do you like this music?" he asked.

I wondered if this was a trick question, but decided to go with the truth. "It's okay."

"Well, then I've got someone you have to meet. What are you doing tomorrow?"

I walked over to the couch and sat down. He sat across from me in the corduroy armchair. Dad's favorite chair.

He wore tan pants with no holes in the knees. A button-down shirt over a gray T-shirt. Almost as if he'd dressed for the occasion. He was rosy. Pink. Maybe he was nervous. Or winded from the walk over here; I'd never seen him with a bike.

The cut on his cheek had healed a bit, and I noticed for the first time a softness about him. He wasn't beautiful like Nick, but there was a sweet, almost cartoonish humor to his look. He had a face you'd throw away the rules for. A face to unlock doors.

"I'm supposed to go to the shop, but . . ." I picked up a cushion and put it in my lap. It was doing nothing to help hide my hideous pajamas. I turned it over a few times and then put it back down again. "How did you know where I live, anyway?"

"I've been following you."

Maybe I shouldn't have opened the door.

He leaned forward and grinned. "Robin. I'm kidding. I knew your address from the inside of your backpack. *If Lost, Please Return to Drew Solo: One Forty-Six Mount Pleasant Drive.*"

Right. My backpack.

"There's a phone number in there too," I said. "You could have called." *You didn't have to wait a whole week.*

"I could have," he said. "But then maybe you'd never have invited me over."

I thought of the bag in the refrigerator.

"Are you hungry?"

"I'm pretty much always hungry."

I led him into the kitchen.

The paper bag held linguini, fresh pesto, and a wedge of Reggiano. Mom didn't believe in pregrating cheese. We always shaved it fresh over our hot plates.

I put water on to boil, took out some silverware and a cloth napkin, and set him a place at the counter. I'd never cooked for anyone other than Mom, and I was nervous.

"What about you?" he asked.

"I ate already."

"So did I. You don't see that stopping me."

It wasn't that the cornflakes had filled me up, it was that when nervous, like a rat, I tended to lose my appetite.

He picked up his fork and twirled it between his fingers.

"Robin, there's something I need to talk to you about."

This sounded serious. I knew the saying about a watched pot never boiling, but I stared at it anyway.

"It's about Hum," he said. "I don't know if you know this about rats, but they should have at least one other rat, a rat to attach themselves to, or else they get lonely."

Hum needed a friend? That was all he wanted to tell me?

Emmett might have thought he knew everything about rats, but he didn't understand that Hum was different. Hum didn't need another rat, because he had me.

"I take him everywhere. He's never alone."

This statement didn't account for the fact that, at that moment, Hum was very much alone in my room. He wasn't allowed in the kitchen when we were cooking or eating. It was one of the rare occasions when Mom's rules actually made some sense.

"Yeah, that's another thing," he said. He leaned back in his stool, almost tipping over. "That cage you take him everywhere in—it's too small. Rats need room to roam."

I put the pasta into the water, which had finally decided to boil. I spun around with a wooden spoon in my hand.

"Is that why you came here tonight? To lecture me about how to take care of my own pet?"

"No, I came here tonight because I like you."

Were there any sayings about watching a pot of water *already* boiling? Because that was what I did. I turned my back to Emmett and stared at the water. I stirred the pasta. It had only a minute more to cook. Not nearly enough time to regain my composure.

"I like you too," I said in a smaller voice than I'd

intended. I meant it, but I wasn't sure I sounded like I did. I was wandering into unfamiliar territory.

At school, with my classmates and friends, I had to decode the hidden meaning of words, to search for what Ms. Bethel in our English class called *intentionality*. There was what people said, and then there was what they were thinking. Take that first lunch at Antonio's when Georgia said *Shut up*, when what she really meant was *Say more*.

One thing I knew for sure was that boys never came out and told girls they liked them, and girls certainly never told this to the boys.

"Good," he said. "I'm glad we got that settled."

I drained the pasta and grated the cheese over it. I slid the plate in front of him. For some reason I felt totally at ease. Even my sheep pajamas seemed less a crime against humanity.

"So will you blow off work and spend the day with me tomorrow?"

"Of course," I said.

"All right!" He put up his hand for a high five and then caught my hand midslap and squeezed it tight. It was friendly. It lasted only a second. And it was the single most romantic moment of my life.

the stolen child

Emmett left only minutes before Mom returned. I felt like I'd dodged a bullet, though I wasn't sure exactly what the bullet was. Beyond unlocking the door, I hadn't done anything wrong, and anyway, I assumed the unlocking-the-door rule pertained to people I didn't know.

I knew Emmett Crane. Even if there were still things I didn't know about him, those were mere details. I knew him.

When I heard the front door open and Mom's footsteps on the stairs I flipped off my bedroom light. I wasn't in bed yet, and I hadn't brushed my teeth or washed my face, but I didn't want to make small talk about balancing ledgers or what I had or hadn't watched on TV, and I certainly didn't want to talk about silver cars. I didn't want to break the magic spell of my night. This night belonged to me.

Just as she reached the top of the stairs I made a dive for

my bed—the early decision to change into those awful pajamas came back to save me—and my head hit the pillow just as my door creaked open.

"Birdie?"

I played statue.

She stood there adjusting to the darkness of my room. She was looking for the shape of me. Making sure that I was still there.

"Love you madly," she whispered.

Emmett showed up at eleven the next day. I watched from my bedroom window, and when I saw him round the corner I raced down the stairs and undid the lock.

I'd dressed all wrong. There he stood in long surf shorts, flip-flops, and a tank top, and I was wearing jeans and sneakers and a hooded sweatshirt. Mom was a big believer in air-conditioning. I had no idea how warm it was out in the real world.

He lifted his sunglasses and checked me out. His look said it all. I ran back upstairs to change.

"To be fair," I called from my bedroom, "you didn't say where we were going."

"I'm pretty sure I didn't say anything about going skiing," he called back. "Or ice fishing."

I put a bathing suit on under a pair of shorts and a T-shirt. I hadn't been anywhere near the beach all summer. It was a crime. I loved the beach, though there wasn't much fun in going alone.

I checked myself in the mirror. I was pasty. I missed the

girl with the raw peeling nose from summers before Mom started the shop, when she'd take me and a few towels, a bucket and shovel, and a magazine or two and we'd spend the whole day by the surf.

I ran down the stairs to meet Emmett, and it wasn't until he mirrored my expression back to me that I realized I was grinning from ear to ear.

"What?"

I couldn't come out and say *I'm happy, really happy, for the first time in a long while*. "Nothing."

"Okay then." He shrugged.

He followed me into the kitchen, where I grabbed some fruit and cheese. He'd brought a backpack too, and we filled his with the food, leaving room in mine for towels, water, and Hum.

Emmett motioned for me to lead the way and he closed the front door behind us.

I always went to lifeguard station 21, where the beach was the widest and the water the calmest. It was the only beach I knew, and I could do the fifteen-minute walk there with my eyes closed. First you had to turn left out the front door, which I did, just as Emmett turned to the right.

We stopped, spun around, and faced each other. It was funny, the choreography of a sitcom. We were both so sure we were in sync we assumed words didn't need to be spoken.

"This way." He waved me toward him.

"Really?" I shot him my most skeptical look.

"I promise."

I shrugged. "Okay then."

I walked toward him and he reached out. I thought he was about to put his arm around me, but instead he gave me a friendly shove and we were on our way.

The walk to Emmett's beach took almost twice as long as the walk to mine, but I held back from pointing this out. I was working on not having to be right all the time. It was the by-product of being an only child, I guessed. In my house there was my room, my stuff, my clothes—I didn't have to share anything, not even ideas and opinions.

I was stubborn. Mom had been telling me so since I was old enough to understand and then reject the label, which of course meant I was being stubborn about being stubborn. She said I inherited this from my father. It was right there on his List of Biggest Flaws in capital letters: *STUBBORNNESS.*

Emmett's beach required that we scramble down some rocks just around the northern bend of a cove. The first thing I noticed was that there wasn't a lifeguard station. I was a good swimmer, maybe even an excellent swimmer, but that didn't mean I didn't need a lifeguard. I believed nobody was above the law of the ocean.

We jumped down from the last rocks onto a small stretch of white sand that backed up to a steep cliff. It was a secret spot of beach, the kind nobody knows about. Nobody except for a group of kids gathered around a table built from two tree stumps spanned by an old surfboard. They were those elusive older, wiser teens. The ones who at school would never give a seventh grader the time of day.

"Emmett!" one shouted. Emmett gave a friendly wave and led me toward them.

Someone had a guitar. But the music stopped as we approached.

"Hey, guys," Emmett said. "This is Robin."

"Robin!" they shouted in unison. I'd never had a group shout my name in unison, never mind that Robin wasn't my name anymore. This day already felt like it was happening to somebody else, so the name suited me just fine.

The guitarist returned to his playing and singing and the others returned to listening and Emmett leaned over toward me and pointed.

"Jasper, Christian, Molly, Deirdre."

Three were smoking cigarettes. Two had tattoos. Molly had a ring in her upper lip.

"And the person I really wanted to you meet," he whispered as he pointed to the guitarist, "is Finn."

Finn was older. He had a beard, for one thing. Strawberry-colored and shaggy. He wore a wool cap over his strawberry hair. His guitar was covered in stickers and his fingers were filled with silver rings.

The song sounded familiar. Like a lullaby, something someone had sung to me once, though Mom wasn't much of a singer.

"Finn's a busker," Emmett said into my ear. I liked the way it sounded even if I didn't know what it meant. "He's from Ireland. He sounds like what you were playing last night, but maybe even better, don't you think?"

I nodded. It wasn't just the music, it was the cliffs, the secrecy, the danger I felt near strangers, the warmth of Emmett's breath in my ear—all of it made me want to lose myself in that song.

I listened. He closed his eyes as he sang.

"Come away, human child!
To the water and the wild
With a faerie hand in hand,
For the world's more full of weeping than you can under-
stand."

It hit me what was familiar about Finn's song. I didn't recognize the tune; I knew the words. They were from a poem by William Butler Yeats.

From Dad's Book of Lists, Favorite Poets: *Shel Silverstein, W. B. Yeats.*

I hadn't heard of Yeats, so one day when things were slow at the shop I'd gone to the library and checked out a collection of his poems. These words were from the one that spoke to me. It was called "The Stolen Child."

Finn stopped. There was a pause and then a round of applause.

"Okay, ladies and gents," Finn said. "Enough from me. Go on about yourselves. Enjoy the day."

He put the guitar away in its case. Jasper, or maybe it was Christian, took Molly, the girl with the ring in her lip, by the hand. They ran into the ocean and fell over backward into the waves. She was wearing cutoff jeans and a white V-neck T-shirt. He had on cargo shorts and a plaid flannel shirt with the sleeves cut off. They came up for air and he grabbed her around the waist. Laughter rolled from the ocean back up to where I stood next to Emmett, wondering what I was doing here.

I would never be that girl. I would never swim where there was nobody certified to rescue me from an undertow. I'd never jump into any body of water fully clothed. I doubted that any boy would ever take my hand like that, run beside me, and then pull me toward him into the waves, laughing, grabbing on tighter.

"That's a good one," Emmett said to Finn. "Top stuff."

"Thanks, little man." Finn squatted down, placing his guitar in its case. He looked up at Emmett, squinting into the sun. "I wonder, though—it might be a tad dark? Not sure it's what folks want to hear when they're shopping for diapers and frozen pizzas."

"Dark is good," Emmett said. "Sad is good. It makes people want to do better."

Finn smiled and finished latching the case. He slung a knitted bag over his shoulder and held his hand out to me. "Robin. It's a pleasure."

He did a little bow then turned to leave. Emmett and I sat down at the surfboard table and watched him scramble up the rocks and disappear. The others were all in the ocean or down at the water's edge. I reached into the sand and buried the cigarette butts they'd dropped right where they'd been standing. Some were still smoldering.

"I wish I had a talent like Finn's," Emmett said. "It's better than money. Or a house. Or a car. Or anything, really. If you've got a talent, if there's something you can do and do it well, all the other stuff will follow."

I didn't want to point out the holes in Finn's knit bag and in his shirt, that it hardly seemed his talent held the door open for great things, but I understood Emmett's

95

point. I wished for that too, for something spectacular about me.

"Where do you know all these people from?" I asked.

"Around."

I recognized this as the kind of answer you give when you're avoiding the question. I recognized it because I'd just started trying this kind of answer out on Mom.

But why was he avoiding *my* question? What was he hiding?

I decided to go with something he wouldn't mind my asking. "What's a busker?" I said.

"Someone who sings for money."

"Isn't that a singer?"

"I guess it's someone who sings for money on the streets. Or in front of the supermarket, which is where Finn tends to do his busking."

"Which supermarket?"

"The Safeway."

We never went to the Safeway anymore. Between what we took home from the shop, Fireside Liquor, and Greenblatt's Grocery two blocks west on Euclid, we covered all the bases. I suddenly missed the aisles of frozen desserts and the cheap plastic toys stacked next to the flu and cold medicines. That was how long it had been since I remembered being there with my mom—since I was young enough to bargain for some crappy toy while pink with fever.

"So that's what he does with his talent? He stands outside the Safeway and sings for spare change?"

"That's what he does *now*," Emmett said. "The Safeway is

a temporary stop. He travels the world on that spare change. He's just earning enough here so he can keep moving on."

Just then the group emerged from the ocean. Molly and the boys who had pulled her into the water shook out their equally shaggy hair.

I'd removed the food from Emmett's backpack and spread it on the surfboard, but I'd left Hum zipped up inside. For one of the first times ever, I felt self-conscious about my rat.

Cigarettes were cool. So were lip piercings. Tattoos. Unguarded swims in the ocean.

Pet rats? About that, I wasn't so sure.

They ate standing up, barely pausing to swallow. Mom always insisted on chairs while eating. If she caught me snacking from the refrigerator she'd yell at me, and because of that, a stolen swig from a carton of milk or a piece of meat pulled from the carcass of a chicken while standing with the cool refrigerated air in my face was one of the most delicious tastes I knew.

With a chorus of *laters* and *see yas*, they departed.

"Cheese rind?" Emmett picked it up and then dropped it.

"No, but I know someone who might find that appetizing."

I freed Hum. He raced up and down the surfboard table-top before he spotted the rind. Maybe Emmett was right about him needing room to roam.

We sat looking out at the ocean. There was just so much of it, and it never failed to take my breath away. Looking at the ocean gave me the same sensation I'd get staring at a sky full of stars—that I was small. Like the way a math problem reveals its undeniable truth, I knew when I stared into this

sort of endlessness that my life didn't count for much of anything. And knowing that, that I was nothing but a speck, I
felt pretty lucky for all that I had.

"Are you thinking about going for a swim?" Emmett
asked.

I laughed. I couldn't have told him what I was really
thinking because I didn't have the words to explain. All I
knew was that I was happy sitting next to him, happy to live
right where I did with this beautiful, endless ocean.

"I'm thinking I'd rather not," I said carefully, not want-
ing to seem too cautious.

"Whew. Me neither."

"Because there's no lifeguard?"

"No. Because I'm a terrible swimmer."

"How come?"

"I never got around to learning." He looked at me. He was
searching my face the way I searched the ocean. "Teach me?"

Nobody had ever asked that of me, that I be the teacher.
I looked away. "Sometime, maybe. Sure. But not here."

We played with Hum. Emmett taught him to fetch. I'd
never have believed Hum capable of such a trick, but he
learned it quickly from the rat master himself. And next, Emmett promised, he'd teach Hum to come when called.

I didn't own a watch and I didn't care about time. There
wasn't anyone or anything waiting for me. It was just another
day at the beach.

Of course, had I known what was happening while I was
sitting at that surfboard table with Emmett, I'd have run all
the way home. Or I'd have never left the house in the first
place. Better yet, I'd have gone in to work that morning.

But all of that was magical thinking. There wasn't anything I could have done to prevent what happened, short of some random act that changed all the random acts that would follow.

I knew the theory about the butterfly flapping its wings in the jungle. How everything happens because of the flapping. But I didn't live in the jungle. I lived in the middle of California on a jagged edge of continent.

I was smaller than a butterfly. I was a speck.

What happened had nothing at all to do with me, with what I did or didn't do, but that wasn't how it felt at the time.

the in-between

He walked me home. I still didn't know if this was on his way or out of his way to wherever it was he lived. There was still so much I didn't know.

When I got to my block I saw Swoozie sitting on the front stairs of our house. This didn't strike me as unusual. My first reaction was to smile. Swoozie had a way of making me feel happy.

For a few seconds I dwelled in that marvelous in-between. In the steps before I reached her, my day was still about a private cove, a boy with a cartoon face, a rat retrieving a macadamia shell, a poem on a guitar. It hadn't yet become *that terrible day*.

"Birdie!" she called. And there it was in the way she said my name, a hysteric lift. The *-ie* rising like a fire alarm.

She stood up and smoothed out her maroon shop apron. She was collecting herself.

She threw her fleshy arms around me.

"There's been an accident."

She released me, took my face into her hands, looked at me with watery eyes.

"It's Nick."

It's terrible to say, but I'll say so anyway, because it's true, and because I punished myself enough for thinking it afterward. What I thought as she spoke those words was: *Thank God.*

It wasn't Mom. Fate hadn't conspired to take both of my parents from me.

Thank God.

Swoozie squeezed me tighter. "He was on his Vespa. He was taking a curve in the road, too fast maybe, I don't know. The tire. The rear one. It blew out."

When Swoozie released me from her grip I turned to Emmett. To pull him in to me like that boy did to Molly in the ocean, to hang on to him as the ground began to disappear from beneath my feet. But I didn't. I couldn't. Because when I turned around to reach for him, he was gone.

indigo night

I stayed home with Swoozie while Mom was at the hospital.

I didn't feel like talking, so I went up to my room. I stared out my window. The sun was going down. The day at the beach had taken place a lifetime ago.

Our street looked deserted. Just how I felt. Mom wasn't home to comfort me. Emmett had disappeared right as I needed someone to reach for. And Nick. Beautiful Nick. Where had he been going? Why had he been in such a hurry? What would happen to him? Was he conscious? Was he in pain? Was he going to be okay? Was he leaving me for good?

Nick had to be okay. Nick was perfection.

Nick was forever.

I leaned out my window as far as I could without losing my balance. It was a balmy indigo night. An in-between color.

I noticed Swoozie's Porsche parked out front. Even the

hood had a dent in it. I wondered why she hadn't parked in our driveway until I looked and saw Mom's car.

I opened my door and went downstairs. Swoozie was sitting on the couch knitting. Right where I'd left her.

"Where's Mom?"

She put down her needles and said gently, "You know she's at the hospital, Birdie. I told you so. Now can I get you some tea? I'm having some with rose hips. I find it calms the nerves."

"Why's her car here?"

"Oh." Swoozie picked up her needles again and went back at the brown and orange mass of yarn in her lap. "She was too upset to drive. She got a ride to the hospital."

I sat down next to her, suddenly seized by exhaustion. I'd gotten too much sun. I should have worn sunblock.

I watched her hands work the needles, and their rhythm and precision lulled me into a state of almost-sleep. My eyes were open, but they weren't seeing, like how when you stare at an object for too long you lose focus and can no longer see it for its shape.

"Are you going to tell me about the boy?"

I sat up. "What boy?" I asked stupidly.

"The boy who hightailed it out of here soon as he saw me."

I stretched out on the couch facing our fireplace and put my head on Swoozie's lap. She moved the yarn out of her way to make room. This position worked. I didn't want to have to look at her, at anyone, and I was so thoroughly tired. I felt like those little kids on TV who fall asleep in the car, or at a party, and are carried to bed in the arms of their fathers.

"His name is Emmett."

"That's nice. Pretty." She picked up my hair and ran it through her fingers. She separated it into strands and slowly began to braid it.

"I should warn you, Birdie," Swoozie said. "Your momma's fit to be tied. She couldn't find you, and you left no note."

"So?"

"So she was distraught. About everything. Maybe it got all jumbled together. When things feel like they're spinning out of control, sometimes you need to fixate on something, and she chose to fixate on where you'd gone. I told her not to worry, that I'd wait here for you, and she should go on to the hospital. But she kept on yelling that you should have left a note."

I thought about getting up and writing one right then and timing it earlier in the day in the top left corner like Mom always did to her notes. Then I could have blamed her for not finding it. It wasn't a bad idea. And I might have done that. But it was too late. Swoozie was working my hair like that yarn and I was losing the battle against sleep.

The slamming of a car door jolted me out of Swoozie's lap. We stood and raced to the front door, opening it to glimpse the taillights of a silver car rounding the corner and Mom walking slowly up the front steps.

She looked pale. Old. Her eyes were bloodshot and puffy.

"He's going to be okay."

Immediately I imagined him walking out of the hospital, sliding glass doors opening for him. I saw him stepping into the shade of the maple trees that lined the street out front.

I saw him looking up into the sun and smiling. I saw him shaking his head like he was casting off a bad dream.

This is not how Nick left the hospital.

He did not walk out the doors because he lost his right leg. But I didn't know this. Mom decided to wait until morning to break the news to me.

I couldn't let myself think about what might have happened had he not gone out and bought that helmet. And he'd never have bought the helmet in the first place had he not fallen in love with Becca. So that day I saw her outside the window in her peasant skirt was the day the butterfly flapped its wings in the jungle. Becca saved Nick's life. She was an angel.

Becca hadn't been with him on the bike. She had a job at a clothing boutique that wasn't as generous with its lunch breaks. Nick had gone off to eat alone. To watch the waves that making fresh pasta kept him from surfing.

She was by his bedside almost every minute of every day that followed. That's where I finally introduced myself to her and she told me how much she'd heard about me, how much Nick loved me.

He loved me.

That night Mom held on to me on our front steps. She took in several deep whiffs of my hair. She whispered to me that she'd worried. That I'd gone and disappeared without leaving a note. That she thought we had an understanding. That she was too tired to argue, but that we'd talk more after getting some sleep.

She went to bed. Swoozie went home. After I'd been so tired, sleep avoided me. I stared at the wallpaper in my room and wondered when it had happened that I'd outgrown it. The circus elephants and colorful balls didn't comfort me or make me feel at home—they served only to remind me of the things I needed to change about my life. Yes. I'd start with the wallpaper.

I turned over. I buried my face in my pillow.

Why had Emmett run away? Why hadn't he said good-bye? Where had he been going? Couldn't he see that something was wrong? Hadn't it occurred to him that maybe I'd need a friend? Did he even understand friendship?

And Nick. Perfect Nick and his lime-green Vespa. I thought of the day he took me for a ride. How I'd climbed on the back without a helmet. Nothing had mattered more than being with him, being seen with him. I'd waved at that school bus even though I knew in my heart nobody was watching.

Nobody cared but me.

done

Swoozie ran the shop for the next few days, and I helped her out. It was better than sitting in the hospital waiting for updates on Nick's surgeries. I tried my best to make pasta. I summoned up everything Nick had taught me. I replayed his lessons. I thought of his patience, his smile, the way he'd make a crater with the flour and crack the eggs into it, the way he took hold of what the pasta machine spat out to check for firmness and width before cutting it to size. While my pasta came out more or less looking right, I knew that it couldn't possibly taste as good as Nick's.

Mom picked up groceries on her way back from the hospital and cooked dinner every night. We didn't say much to each other. Mom was tired. I didn't want to know the details. I couldn't bear the thought of his leg. What do you do with a lost leg? Where does a leg go that is all done living?

Luckily, Mom didn't seem to want to talk much either, so we ate in silence, with only the melancholy sounds of her favored Irish folk record in the background.

At night in my room I held Hum in my lap and I reread Dad's Book of Lists. I knew it by heart, yet somehow I hoped I'd find a new list somewhere in its pages. A list of ways to fight back, or grab on tighter, when it felt like everything was slipping away.

I started the project of removing my wallpaper. I peeled it slowly and only in the spots behind my dresser or the headboard of my bed so that Mom couldn't see what I was up to.

And while I was alone in my room at night, I began my own list.

A list of Things That Are Suddenly Clear:

Mom is dating somebody.

Whoever drove that silver car was close enough to Mom to be there when she was too upset to drive herself. Who does this for you but someone who loves you? Someone who you love back?

I don't know Emmett Crane.

Or at least, he wasn't who he claimed to be, not that he claimed much about himself. The boy I thought I knew would have come back to check on me. He wouldn't let so much time go by.

I'd watched enough TV in the lonely afternoons after school, before there was a cheese shop to go to, to know that there were boys who lied, who knew how to say just the right thing or give you just the right look. Boys who could make you feel a way you thought you didn't deserve to feel.

So I was done.

Done with him. Done with feeling. Done with the beating of my heart.

the jingle of the bell

By the next week things were starting to feel like a new version of normal. Mom had returned to the shop. Swoozie had hired a replacement for Nick. "Only temporary," she said. "Until Nick gets back on his foot again."

Maybe because it was too early to joke, or maybe because this girl was not Nick yet took over most of his tasks with ease, I hated her at first sight.

Her name was Veronica and she was reedy and tall, with a short dark bob, severe bangs, and a permanent whisper of a voice. I'd like to say that she was mean, or cold, or at the very least indifferent, because that would justify why I was so rude to her, but she was tremendously sweet. She also knew her food. The daughter of two chefs from New York City, she'd come to the Central Coast for its bounty. Mom had once told me that we grew about one-fifth of all the nation's food, but I never quite believed that, because I was too committed to the idea that nothing about where I lived mattered to the rest of the world.

Nick was still in the hospital, and would be there for weeks to work with a team of physical therapists. One afternoon I brought along a batch of egg linguini, the most basic fresh pasta, not because I thought he could eat it, but because I wanted him to check out my handiwork. To see what I'd been doing while he'd been gone. How I'd chosen to honor him.

Becca stood up as I came in. She motioned for me to sit in the chair by his bed, the one she rarely left empty, but I walked over to the window and sat on the sill.

"I'm going for a coffee," she said. "Can I get you anything?"

I thought about asking for a latte, but I shook my head no. "How 'bout you, baby?"

He smiled at her, a little sadly. "A right leg?"

She put her hand on his cheek. "With cream and sugar?" He closed his eyes against the kiss she placed on his forehead. He watched her leave the room.

Nick's mother had offered to fly in from Argentina, but he said she didn't need to, so she wasn't coming. This made no sense to me. What kind of mother doesn't come when her son loses his leg?

I handed him the egg linguini. He took a strand and gave it a tug. Held it up to the light. He took the tiniest bite, even though uncooked pasta tastes like clay.

"Come here." He motioned me over from the window where I was keeping my distance. It had no view. I wished more than anything that he could see the ocean from his hospital bed. The waves he loved so.

He grabbed me by the wrist and pulled me closer. He gave me something in between a hug and a noogie. "Don't get any better at this, kiddo, or I'll be out of a job."

He'd lost his leg, so somehow I expected that he'd look different, that he'd act different, but he was still every bit the Nick I knew.

"I'm really sorry." I took a long swallow. "So, so sorry this had to happen to you."

"This?" he asked, and he lifted up his pale blue hospital blankets, took a peek underneath. He sighed. "At least I've still got a good one."

I don't know why his resilience surprised me. He was unflappable Nick. Nothing rattled his world. Like that day of the health inspection, he always saw things for the way they could be fixed.

People talk about the reserves you never know you have until you call upon them. But I'd done a little poking around for mine. They weren't hiding anyplace. I could never recover from an accident like Nick's. Or from my husband's death while I had a small child to raise.

I couldn't even seem to put the disappearance of Emmett behind me. I told myself that it didn't matter in a world where Nick was in the hospital and Mom was keeping a major secret from me, but the disappointment sat like a balloon filled with sand somewhere in my middle. I felt it whenever I took a deep breath.

So I avoided deep breathing. No dramatic sighs. No sitting down at the end of the day and putting my feet on the couch. At night I stayed up too late watching TV that didn't interest me.

Right when I'd almost convinced myself that he didn't matter, that the summer would end, my friends would return from England, I'd start eighth grade, Nick would come back and work the pasta machine from a wheelchair, business would pick up, Mom wouldn't worry about work or lie about where she was going at night, he returned.

He didn't leave a note in the alley.

Or show up at my house when he knew nobody else was at home.

This time, the bell jingled as he walked right through the front door into the Cheese Shop.

looking for somebody

Veronica greeted him with her whisper voice.

"May I help you?"

He didn't see me sitting in the pasta corner. Veronica had ceded it to me and taken up work behind the cash register.

"Yeah, I'm just . . ." He turned and our eyes locked. ". . . looking for somebody."

I went back to the mixing bowls. I'd lost track of the number of eggs I'd cracked, so I tried retracing my steps by counting the broken yolks.

"Hey," he said.

"Hey." I didn't look up. *Six yolks. Seven.*

"Can you take a break?"

"No."

"Just a minute?"

"I'm working."

"I can wait."

"I'm busy."

"Robin." I looked up. For some reason it was important that nobody hear him call me that. "I'm sorry."

Just then Mom came out from her office in the back. She started walking toward us and I thought I could see in Emmett's face, and in a slight jerk of his body, the desire to flee. But he stood there and he shook Mom's hand.

"I'm Lizzie," she said. "Drew's mom."

"I'm Emmett. Her friend."

"Yes." She studied his face. "Drew tells me you're a big fan of our cheese."

His cheeks flushed. I stepped into him, became him for an instant, and understood what it was that made him redden. He thought I'd told Mom that he took our cheese and day-old food from the alley. He thought I'd betrayed him.

I would never do that. I caught his eye. *Never,* I tried telling him with my look. *I would never betray you.*

Mom put an arm around him, the way she did with me, with the few friends I'd brought home over the years. "Here," she said. "Try something new. We just got this in this morning."

She led him over to the case and selected a cheese, handing it to Veronica to slice. I was too far into making my pasta to walk away without ruining the entire batch. But I watched, and I saw the ease with which Emmett took the cheese from Mom and how he returned her smile, and I knew that whatever worry he might have had that I'd told his secrets was gone.

Anyway, it was Emmett who'd betrayed me. He'd disappeared when I needed a friend. Right then, whether he knew it or not, he was the only real friend I had.

And he'd left me.

Mom returned to her office and Emmett to my corner.

"Can you take a break?"

I turned on the pasta machine and dumped in my mixture.

"No."

"I thought that's what you'd say."

He dug his hand into the pocket of his jeans with the holes in the knees. "I don't blame you."

He pulled out a wad of paper and then took it in his fingers and reshaped it, smoothed it out, and did a final few small folds before placing it on the counter next to me. Another crane.

"Goodbye."

I didn't look up or say a word; I just waited for the sound of the bell behind him.

Something told me I didn't want to read his note at work, where Mom or Swoozie or Veronica might see me. So I waited. And I was right to wait, because when I got home that night, and went up to my room and closed my door and opened the crane and read his note, I started to cry.

what it said inside the paper crane

I want to be your friend, but I'm afraid I don't know how.

someone like me

I cried.

And cried.

I felt confused. Bewildered. Not just by his note and what it meant, but also by the hurricane of emotion it stirred in me. I cried for Nick and his paper-thin hospital blanket. I cried for the fifty-two pages that made up Dad's Book of Lists, a life in a deck of cards, the weeks in a year. I cried for Mom and her calculator ribbon of worry. I cried for the silver car that drove her away from me.

I took Emmett's note apart and put it back together again. Not just folding and refolding the paper, but folding and refolding his words, reshaping them, trying to understand them. Searching for his *intentionality*.

Was he afraid he didn't know how to be my friend because I made that too hard on everyone? I looked at my list of friends. Stephania Allessio, Aaron Finklestein, Alison

Samuel. Georgia, Beatrice, and Janice. Any way you cut it, it was a pathetic list. Thirteen years. Six people.

Or maybe it was Emmett who had the hard time with friendship? But if it was, then how could I explain Jasper, Christian, Molly, and Deirdre? Or Finn? He had friends. Older friends. He had friends the way I had Nick and Swoozie.

I went into the bathroom and washed my face. I held a cold cloth to my eyes. I looked at my puffy reflection in the mirror.

I want to be your friend, but I'm afraid I don't know how.

I could have written that same note.

I'd met someone like me. After all this time. Someone just like me. And I'd let him walk away. Literally. Bell jingling behind him.

I went back to my room and looked at my clock. Eleven-thirty.

Even with a closet full of reflector vests, I knew enough not to leave home at that hour. And even if I could, even if I could will myself that sort of courage, I didn't have the first idea of where to go looking for him at an hour like that.

So I went to sleep. And I dreamed of lists. Of all the things I'd say when I found him. All the ways I'd make him my first real friend.

so vital

I woke up early. Mom was still home. She sat at the breakfast table with her ledger, writing checks.

"Am I hallucinating?" she asked. "Is this really you? My daughter? Up before the lunch hour?"

She poured herself another cup of coffee.

"Morning," I said.

"It is."

I sat down and reached for her toast, and she swatted my hand away.

"I'm taking the day off," I said.

"Really?" She took a sip, not looking up from her book. "Because I'm not sure this is such a great time. What with Nick gone and Veronica still learning the ropes, we need all the help we can get."

I was torn. Mom was finally willing to admit she needed me, but she also assumed I had nothing better to do with my time.

"Sorry, Mom. I've got things I need to do today."

She put down her pen and closed her book. She fixed me with her tired eyes.

"What could possibly be so *vital?*"

"Why does everything have to be vital? I just can't come to work. I've got other stuff to do."

"Like what?"

"Like stuff."

"That's not going to cut it, Drew. I need to know where you're going."

This was debris, left over from that horrible night of Nick's accident. She was still mad at me for not being home and for not telling her where I was, and I knew she was mad only because she had to be mad at someone. Some*thing.* Because Nick's Vespa had spun out and hit a tree, and you can't get mad, or stay mad, at a tree.

"This is *my* business," I said.

"No, Drew. You don't have your own business. I need to know where you're going."

"You have *your* own business. And I don't mean the Cheese Shop."

"I know what you mean. And I don't think I like your tone."

I held my breath. I counted to five. It was the first time I made it all that way, so I counted to ten. I still didn't know what to say.

The truth wasn't an option because I didn't know the truth. I didn't know where I'd go looking for Emmett, but more than that, I didn't know why he felt like the most important thing in the universe, why he felt so *vital*, and I didn't know why Mom was the last person I felt I could ask why that might be so.

We were building a wall between us, Mom and me.

"Listen, Birdie." She reached for my hand. "Do you want to talk about the—"

"No," I snapped. I didn't want to hear about Mom's life, about the silver car. I didn't want to know anything. I just wanted her to leave me alone.

She put her hands up in mock defense.

"I don't know what I'm going to do today. I just know I don't want to be at the shop. I have a life. My own life that doesn't involve selling cheese."

"Wonderful."

Mom so rarely turned on the sarcasm that it stung when she did.

"No, really, this is just terrific." She stood up and took her dishes to the sink. "I guess it was inevitable that you start pulling this teenage crap on me."

"Whatever, Mom. Go complain about me to your boyfriend."

She stopped and spun around. She looked at me with the same sort of bewilderment I'd felt in my room the night before. Then she took in a deep breath through her nose, yoga style, and walked out of the kitchen and through the front door, slamming it behind her, without counting to five.

"Who do you think is going to wash these dishes?" I yelled after her. "Last time I checked we had no cleaning staff!"

have you seen me?

I started with the cove, even though the day was cloudy. I
rode my bike as far as I could, and I left it leaning against a
telephone pole as I jogged down the beach to the rocks and
scrambled over them. Empty. I walked over to the surfboard
table and ran my hands up and down it, sweeping the cigarette butts into the sand and then burying them.

I rode over to Capri Drive and the beginning of the trail
to Garfield Park. The brush had been cleared a bit, and I
wondered whether Mrs. Mutchnick had finally worn down
the fire marshal. I'd planned on hiking up the hill but was
suddenly worried about being on my own. Even ignoring the
threat of fire, there were still snakes.

I decided to go ahead anyway, but after a few strides another idea struck. I turned around, climbed back on my bike,
and pedaled as fast as I could in the opposite direction. I
coasted down the hill, crossed Euclid Ave, rode by the library, the elementary school, the gas station. I rode by the

hospital and looked up in the vain hope of finding Nick's room, waving to him, having him cheer me on, but I knew his window only looked onto another building. And maybe it was best, I thought, to have no view. Maybe it didn't help to look outside and see people walking, or running, or pedaling furiously on their bikes.

I rode until I reached parking lot of the Safeway, so filled up with cars you'd have thought the threatened nuclear war was finally upon us. *So this is where all the customers go,* I thought. *This is where they're buying tonight's supper.*

I left my bike in the rack and hooked my helmet over the handle. Despite the many safety precautions I took, I never carried a lock. I trusted humanity enough to believe that nobody would steal my bike. Also there was the sad truth that it wasn't worth very much.

I didn't see Finn at either entrance, so I stepped inside. I knew I wouldn't find him busking by the vegetables and waxy fruit, but I wanted to be thorough. I wanted to leave no stone unturned.

I wandered the aisles. When I reached the pasta section I saw varieties even I'd never even heard of, all dried, of course, and I knew the difference between dried and fresh, but still, with so much to choose from and with prices a fraction of ours, no wonder the parking lot was full. No wonder Mom was losing sleep.

I bought myself a packet of string cheese. The irony wasn't lost on me that of all the foods in the store, I chose the one thing I could get for free at a far superior quality. We didn't carry string cheese. It was an overprocessed, cheap American invention, one that couldn't be imported or purchased from local dairy farms. But it also happened to taste delicious; it reminded me of being a little kid back before I knew about good cheeses, and I devoured all six pieces sitting on the curb at the edge of the parking lot, where I could see both front entrances.

He arrived around one-thirty. I didn't notice which direction he'd come from because I'd been battling boredom by counting the cars in the parking lot and working out what percentage of them was silver.

By the time I saw Finn he was leaning against the shopping cart rack, tuning his guitar. A knit wool cap lay in front of him to collect spare change.

I wandered over, ready to reintroduce myself, but he said, "Hey, Robin."

"Hey," I said as casually as I could.

"What brings you to the Safeway on such a lovely summer's day?"

"String cheese." I held up the wrapper.

"Ah, the cheese of the string," he said as he plucked a few notes on his guitar. He closed his eyes and he began to sing.

"I've searched the world over from Galway to Dover
And delighted in many a thing,
The touch of a lover, the warm breeze of summer,
But nothing, no nothing, no nothing . . ."

He held the note, his voice wavering, before popping his eyes open again, doubling the tempo, and finishing with:

". . . delights like the cheese of the string!"

I applauded. He bowed.

"Did you just make that up?" I asked stupidly.

"No, that's a famous Irish song about string cheese. I learned it from my da. Who learned it from his da." He smiled, letting me know he wasn't mocking me. "And so on."

"Well, it's a keeper," I said. "And you should take a cut of whatever business the Safeway does in string cheese sales."

"Great idea. I'll talk to my manager."

An awkward silence followed.

"I was wondering"—I looked down at my feet—"if maybe you'd know where I might be able find Emmett."

He studied me. Even though I thought I'd done a pretty good job acting as if this question meant little to me, I could see that he understood I hadn't come here for the string cheese.

"I don't know where he lives," I added.

"You don't?"

"No."

"Hmmmm." He picked again at his guitar strings.

I hoped he wasn't about to launch into another song. I was no longer in a mood for his silliness.

"Listen, Robin." He stopped and shifted his guitar to his back, a rainbow strap across his chest. "If Emmett hasn't told you himself, I'm afraid it's not my place."

"Well, I know he lives with his dad and that they're staying on someone's couch or something while they look for their own place to live. They're just getting settled and . . ."

It wasn't until I heard myself say this out loud that I understood that not a word of it was true.

". . . and that's what he told me. . . . He told me they were looking for a bachelor pad."

Finn stared, unblinkingly.

"But none of that is true," I said.

He plucked a few more strings.

I knew there was something more to Emmett's story, even if I hadn't looked too closely. Something that would lead him to the back alley of the Cheese Shop. I didn't have a father, and I guessed fathers didn't send their children out to gather cast-off food, but I'd figured times were really tough for the two of them. That was why they'd come here. Why they were staying with friends on a couch. Times were tough. Tough for everybody.

But still. Something about his story wasn't right.

Emotions whipped through me, pinball style. Stupid: *ding.* Angry: *ding.* Confused: *ding.* Sad and sorry: *ding, ding, ding.*

I sat down on the sidewalk. Right there in front of the Safeway. Finn sat next to me and folded his legs beneath him.

"If you hang around here long enough," Finn said, "he'll probably turn up. He usually pops by in the afternoon."

"I don't know. . . . Maybe I should just go."

"I wouldn't mind the company."

I looked up from the sidewalk, where I was scratching at a patch of dirt. He meant it. He wouldn't mind my company. That was worth something.

"What about you?" I asked.

"What about me?"

"What's your story?"

"I'll tell you mine if you tell me yours."

"I don't have a story. I'm just a normal kid who does what

she's told and never gets in too much trouble. I don't go any-where or do much of anything, and maybe the worst part is that it's never really bothered me."

"Ah. I bet there's more to you than that."

"Maybe. I *would* like to go to Hawaii."

"For the beaches?"

"And the candy bars."

He gave me a puzzled look, but then shrugged it off.

"I'm on my way to Alaska," he said.

"For real?"

"For real."

"Wow."

I didn't know anyone who'd been to Alaska, and I couldn't imagine why anyone would ever want to go. Snow everywhere you looked. Ice houses. Frozen earth. A distant and vanishing sun. So bleak.

"What's in Alaska?" I knew it had to be some shining light in all that darkness. Something *vital.*

"What else?" he said. "A girl." Again, the sound of ran-dom strings plucked while lost in thought. "*The* girl."

We sat by the shopping carts as he told me the story of Lorelai, how they'd met back in Dublin while she was on a school trip, and though they'd only known each other a few days, he loved her, he loved her so completely that the only thing that mattered to him was reaching her again.

Someone threw a few coins into Finn's hat, still resting in front of us. We must have looked like ordinary beggars.

He told me he swore he'd find her. Those were his part-ing words to Lorelai. He promised he'd find her again.

"Let me get this straight," I said. "You haven't spoken to her since?"

"Nary a whisper."

"How long ago was this?"

"Last summer."

"That's a year ago."

"Aye. Alaska is a far way from Dublin. It's a very, very long trip."

"Do you know where she lives?"

"Juneau. Lovely word, isn't it?"

There were questions I wanted to ask. Why hadn't he called her? What if she'd moved on? What if she loved somebody else? What if she *remembered* him, the way you do someone who's gone, but didn't *imagine* him, the way you do when the whole world is still full of possibility?

Soon we were joined by some of the others from the beach. Molly and Christian and Jasper with their dangling cigarettes.

Just as they approached, Finn leaned in close. He whispered, "When there's something, or someone, when there's anything that makes you happy, you don't let a continent or an ocean or an empty pocket keep you apart."

He returned to his busking and we all hung around and listened. A few times Molly joined in and harmonized. It was no wonder that his hat filled quickly. Finn had amazing talent. His voice was a golden ticket. A pass to wherever he wanted or needed to go.

Eventually my backpack started to jump around in quick fits and starts. Hum, up from a power nap, was hungry. I felt a surge of guilt for not saving him a cheese stick, so I ducked back into the Safeway to buy a bag of macadamia nuts.

The day had turned into a scorcher, so I went to the dairy aisle to cool off. I looked at the pathetic selection of cheeses. Business just had to get better at the Cheese Shop. Sure, nothing beats a cheese stick, but who doesn't want a quality imported goat cheddar now and then?

The woman next to me reached for a carton of milk and changed her mind. She returned it to the shelf backward so the carton showed the face of a girl, the words *Have You Seen Me?* below her picture.

I stared at her. I grabbed another carton and looked at its other side. A different girl. Older. Missing since November. I grabbed another: a boy with blond hair and a gap between his teeth. I turned the cartons around, one after another. I felt feverish, on a wild hunt. I dug my arms into the depths of the case. I searched every single one.

Searching for Emmett.

I knew, with a strange, unfamiliar certainty, that Emmett was missing. He was a runaway. It all made sudden, perfect sense.

Have You Seen Me?

Yes, I've seen you. You are missing.

I grabbed the last carton in the case. A boy. Curly dark hair. Kind eyes. Sweet smile.

Not Emmett Crane.

I paid for my nuts and stumbled back into the sunlight. I sat down with the group and let Hum eat out of my hand.

I tried to make some sense of what I'd discovered. I hadn't found him, and yet . . . I knew. The carefully avoided answers. The sudden disappearing acts. The food retrieved from the alley. The misfit band of friends.

Emmett Crane. A runaway.

Why? From what?

I didn't see Mom arrive, but suddenly she was there, arms folded, glaring at me, and for some reason the first thing I did was shove Hum back into my bag. That's what I thought contorted her face—that she'd caught me out of the house with my rat, connected the dots, and realized I took him everywhere, even to the Cheese Shop.

Of course now I can see things as she did. I can imagine what it was like for Mom to approach the grocery store to find her daughter loitering out front with a group of chain-smoking tattooed teenagers scrounging for money.

"Drew?" she said as if she didn't know me. Or hadn't seen me in years. As if she needed to check her senses—make sure her eyes weren't playing tricks on her.

"Drew?" said Jasper. "Who's Drew?"

"Hey, Mom," I said, starting to scramble up, trying to get out of there as quickly as possible.

"Robin?" Molly looked at me.

Mom looked at Molly. Confusion settled on everyone's face but mine, which was turning red. I was caught in a lie that felt much larger than it actually was.

"Let's just go," I said. "Okay, Mom?"

She turned and started walking quickly toward the car. I trailed after her. I waved over my shoulder at Finn and the others and I could see what looked like pity in the way they waved back.

We snaked our way through the parking lot and all those cars. When we reached ours Mom put her hand on the door handle.

"I meant to buy some steaks," she said in a shaky voice. "For dinner."

"Just open the car. Please."

"I need to go buy steaks."

"I don't need meat, Mom. Pasta is fine. Please. Let's just get out of here."

We climbed into our seats and she started the engine. It wasn't until we were driving past the hospital that she spoke again.

"Who are *those people?*"

I looked up in another attempt at spying Nick, like he was a presence in the sky, a benevolent god, rather than an amputee trapped in a hospital bed. *Nick.* He'd know what to do. He'd know how to find Emmett. He'd know why I cared so much. He'd be able to explain those milk cartons to me. He'd know what to say to Mom, how to talk to her about everything that had launched a sneak attack on what was to be my perfect summer.

Nick. He could fix anything.

"Those people," I said, "are my friends." This wasn't entirely true. Okay, so maybe it wasn't true at all, but it felt good to say it. It felt important. *I* felt important.

"They smoke cigarettes."

"So does Swoozie."

"You're thirteen."

"Why are you always reminding me of my age? Like I could ever possibly forget how old I am? I mean, how could I ever forget when you remind me every minute of every day?"

She gripped the wheel tighter. "Why do those people, *your friends*, call you Robin?"

"Because. That's my name."

"Your name is Drew."

"No, Mom. *His* name was Drew. And now he's dead."

Right then I wanted to cry. I wanted to, but I didn't, because the inside of that car no longer felt like a safe place to do so. I'd cried more times in Mom's car than I could possibly count—after school when I felt like my teacher had been picking on me, when there was a birthday party I'd been excluded from, when the sad ending of the movie we'd seen had taken its time creeping up on me. But now I just sat and endured her silence.

I didn't dare look at her. I'd denounced my name. And I'd said the word *dead*.

We pulled into the driveway and she turned off the ignition. She stared straight ahead.

"I guess," she said, "that there are some things we need to talk about."

"There's nothing I want to talk about." As if that weren't harsh enough, I added, "At least, there's nothing I want to talk about *with you*."

I got out of the car and slammed the door. I started walking toward the house.

She unrolled her window.

"Is this all because I've been seeing someone?"

I stopped. I didn't turn around.

"Is that why you're acting this way? Because I've dared to spend some of my free time with someone who isn't you? Grow up, Drew."

"That's exactly what I'm trying to do," I shouted. "But you won't let me."

grounded

Here's the note I found by the kitchen sink the next morning:

7:54 a.m.

DREW Robin Solo—

Do not even think about leaving this house today. You are grounded. You may come to work if you wish, but if you choose not to, you may not leave this house. I will call you at 10:00. And I will continue to call you every hour on the hour all day long to confirm that you are home.

Don't argue. That's the way it has to be.

Mom

The space above where she'd written *Mom* glared at me, an angry, punishing white. No *love you madly*, not even its poor cousin, the simple, lonely *love*. I knew she meant business. I glanced at the clock: 9:39.

I had time for a shower. Showers always helped me think. I stood in them far longer than it took to get clean, staring at my feet until I turned pink. But when I stepped out of this shower, I had no idea how to go about my day, or my life.

The phone rang a minute later.

"I'm here."

"Good."

"Talk to you in an hour." I hung up.

The phone rang again.

"Don't hang up on me."

"I thought we were through."

"We were."

"So?"

"It's customary to say goodbye."

"Goodbye, Mom."

"Goodbye, Birdie."

I let her hang up first this time. I got dressed even though I wasn't going anyplace. How do you dress for a day of nothing? Of exile from the world for crimes you can't even name?

I put on a tank top and a pair of Mom's old yoga pants. I cleaned Hum's cage and I cleaned my room. I took out Emmett's notes, with their crane creases, and reread them, though I knew them by heart, before putting them back in my bedside drawer.

The phone rang again.

"An hour already?" I said.

"Time flies when you're grounded."

"And see? I'm still here."

"Yes, you are. Good girl."

"Don't talk to me like a child."

Mom sighed. "I know you're growing up, Drew. But I want you to know that I'm not taking my eyes off you."

"That sounds creepy."

"I guess what I mean to say is, I'm not falling asleep on the job. I know I've been distracted. Running a business is all-consuming even in the best of times, and Lord knows these have not been the best of times. And yes, I've met someone. When it rains it pours, I suppose. I know I could have handled this better. I should have talked to you earlier, but I wanted to wait until I knew it was something worth telling you about. And now I've gone and messed this up. But we'll figure it out. I promise. We'll sit down and we'll talk. I'm not forgetting you, Drew. You come first. Before anything else in my life. For better or worse."

"Can I go now?"

"Yes, you can go now. Goodbye, love."

"Goodbye, Mom."

I continued my cleaning frenzy. At least, that was how I justified rifling through the piles of mess in Mom's bedroom. Mountains of books abandoned in the middle; clean shirts pulled from the closet, then tossed to the floor; mugs of half-drunk coffee—an anthropologist dropped in the center of Mom's bedroom would have no choice but to conclude that whatever creature inhabited this space suffered from some sort of attention deficit disorder. But I knew that already. Mom had trouble finishing things. That wasn't what I was looking to discover about her.

I wanted to know who drove that silver car.

I looked in her bedside drawer, trying not to think about how awful it was to do that. If Mom went looking through *my* bedside drawer, I'd never forgive her. I'd cease loving her madly. But I opened the drawer anyway, slowly, as if this somehow absolved me of my sin, and I found nothing. No folded and refolded notes. No book of lists including *Men I'm Currently Dating*.

The phone rang again.

"It's only eleven-forty-two," I said. "You're early."

"Robin?"

I pulled the phone away from my ear and stared at it. Then I held it up again.

"Hello . . . Hello . . . ?" he was saying.

Have you seen me?

He must have heard me breathing, because he began to talk. "Please," he said. "Don't hang up. Just listen to me. I want to come see you. Can I come see you? I'm only a few blocks away."

I closed my eyes and traced a circle around my small house, and then I traced another, and another, radiating out, wider and wider, until I could picture a pay phone. Outside Patrick O'Malley's. The bar nobody ever seemed to go into or out of, which was no more than five blocks away.

"I'm grounded," I said.

"I'll come to you." He paused. *"If Lost, Please Return to Drew Solo: One Forty-Six Mount Pleasant Drive."*

All those circles, like rings on a tree stump revealing how long that tree has been alive, and I was the center. My little house. My little life.

"Okay." I hung up without saying goodbye.

You are lost. I stared at the phone tucked back into its cradle.

But I have seen you.

this is not a dream

Mom's twelve o'clock phone call and Emmett's knock on the door arrived simultaneously.

I reached for the phone first. "Can't talk now, on a cleaning jag."

"Don't forget the fridge," she said.

"Goodbye."

"Good—"

I hung up and then worried she'd call again with a lecture about how it isn't customary to cut off somebody in the middle of a goodbye, but she didn't. It was a work in progress, this business of learning how to say goodbye to each other.

I opened the door and stood facing him. I hadn't decided if I was going to let him in or not.

"Robin," he said.

"I know," I said. "I know you aren't staying on a couch with your father and I know you aren't looking for a bachelor pad and I know you ran away from home, wherever that is."

He dug his hands into his pockets and sighed.

Something about the sadness on his cartoon face tipped my inner scales. I let him in. He followed me into the kitchen, where we both sat on stools at the counter.

"I'm not sure where to begin," he said.

I thought of saying *How about at the beginning?* or *How about starting with the truth?* but both of those responses felt cliché to me even then, like something from one of the bad TV shows I liked to watch.

"Start with your name," I said. "Your *real* name."

"Michael Emmett Forsythe."

"So where'd you get Crane from?"

He reached into his pocket and pulled out a paper crane, put it on the counter between us, and shrugged.

"I see."

A long silence followed.

"I'm sorry I lied to you," he said. "You know . . . I can't really come out and tell just anyone that I ran away from home. What if you called the police? What if you thought you were doing the right thing? You're like that, Robin. You want to do the right thing."

I thought about how I'd searched Mom's bedside drawer. How I'd stolen Dad's Book of Lists. How I sneaked Hum into all the places he wasn't allowed. What could possibly have made Michael Emmett Forsythe see me as someone who wanted to do the right thing?

"I don't even know what to call you," I said.

"Call me Emmett. Please."

"Okay."

"People don't run away for no reason, you know. I have my reasons."

"I know. I'm sorry."

I started rifling through the fridge. Mom wasn't kidding. It needed a good clean. I took out bread and salami, turkey, lettuce, mustard, mayonnaise, a jar of gherkin pickles. I'd been raised to believe that something good to eat makes everything better.

I spread the goods out between us while he began to talk.

"Do you ever have dreams about when you were little? You know, like you're in your room and the light is soft, and you're sitting on the carpet and you're playing with your favorite toy, and everything just feels perfect? Like you're really happy?"

I nodded because I sort of knew what he meant, although in my dream, I'm sitting in the lap of a father I don't really remember, leaning against his chest, listening to his heartbeat, while he rattles off a long list of all the things we'll do together someday.

"Well, I can't really tell anymore what's a memory and what's just a dream. I'd like to say that there was a time everything was good. That there was a time when I was happy. But I might have made all that up." He took a slice of salami and popped it in his mouth. "I can tell you this, though. I used to have a real family. A mom and a dad and a little brother. And we used to live in a house where we grew cucumbers in the backyard. They had these little spikes on the outside, so they made for killer weapons if you happened to be into battling like Conan the Barbarian." He smiled at me. "Don't judge."

This, I thought, *is memory.*

This is not a dream.

"And my brother, he's younger than me. His name is David. He shared my room. We only had two, so there was really no choice, but I didn't mind. I never liked sleeping alone. I used to tell him stories in his crib. After my parents shut out the lights. Usually about Conan the Barbarian."

He'd started making a sandwich, but he stopped halfway through.

"Those were happy times. When I thought my stories were putting him to sleep. This was before we realized that he probably wasn't able to understand what I was saying, or much of anything else."

He looked from his half-built sandwich to me.

"I don't mean to blame David. None of what happened is his fault. But when you've just got a small house you rent with a cucumber patch in the back and one parent who works fixing cars but doesn't have health insurance and you discover that there's something wrong with the three-year-old who hasn't learned to talk, things can kind of go to crap."

I remember what I used to tell myself when I was younger: all that business about how lucky I was to have only Mom and me. Magical thinking. Like building a moat around a dream castle.

But maybe I wasn't too far off. Maybe magical thinking can come true.

"It's hard, dealing with the sort of problems David has. As he got older, he seemed to get worse. Stories didn't soothe him to sleep. Not much calmed him down. Not much, other than being with animals. So . . . we got him a pet rat."

Immediately I pictured Hum. Upstairs. Sound asleep in his newly cleaned cage.

"And while rats may be one of earth's most perfect creatures," he said, "they can't make miracles."

He went quiet. I didn't move, even though my feet had fallen asleep. Pins and needles. I felt them everywhere.

"So, Robin. That's my story. The beginning of it, anyway. Have you ever noticed how most stories, at least the ones you learn when you're a kid, start out sad but have happy endings? Well, mine starts out happy, and I'm just doing what I can to keep it from ending on the sad."

I thought of my story. A redheaded father who'd grown a Fu Manchu, who wanted to climb Mount Kilimanjaro, who hated the Doors, who loved his wife and his little Birdie, and who, despite all these passions and desires and convictions, possessed a body that was all done living.

A sad story. But one that would wind up happy: with a girl, her mother, a rat, and some really excellent cheese.

"So what are you trying to do? Why are you running away?" I asked.

He considered me with his kind eyes, the same way he did that first night when I asked why he was in the alleyway. As if I'd asked the simplest question in the universe.

"I'm looking to make a miracle," he said.

the onion fields

We all have our stories. The ones we're told or read as children that never leave us. For me, that story is *Charlotte's Web*, and it always struck me how Emmett mentioned it the very first night we met in the alley, as if he'd removed a big fat crayon from his pocket and drawn a line connecting us together.

Mom first read it to me when I was five, and I began to realize, as she doled out the chapters night after night, that Charlotte was going to die. It made no difference to me that she'd left behind her masterpiece, the sac of spider eggs that would survive her. What good was a world to Wilbur, or to the spiders those eggs would become, without a Charlotte in it?

For Emmett, that story, the one that would not leave him, was a legend.

It wasn't Conan the Barbarian, though he loved that story too. The story Emmett carried with him came from a book of Native American legends his father would read to him and his brother David before it became clear that David wasn't listening, and before David's problems grew too large for their family and the house with the cucumber patch, and before his father ran away, though his face would never appear on a milk carton.

Those were the times Emmett was happiest. When his father would squeeze himself into Emmett's bed with the book of legends, and Emmett would look at their feet side by side and wonder how his would ever grow so big. The book had been his father's when he was a boy, and his favorite legend became Emmett's too. Emmett demanded it every night.

He told me all this as I rode on the handlebars of my bike while he pedaled it behind me. I'd seen other kids doing it, and while they looked like they were having fun—and even more than that, they looked part of a twosome, close enough to share one bike—I always thought it was crazy. Dangerous.

But we had only one hour for Emmett to show me where he'd been living and get me back home in time for Mom's two p.m. call. And anyway, I had my helmet. I hated that I didn't have one to offer him, but he said he was a good cyclist. He promised to deliver us there and home again safely.

He didn't hesitate when I'd asked. He said, *Yes. Of course. There are no more secrets. I'll show you where I've been living.*

At first I thought maybe it was the cove. But I started to realize he was just skirting town, taking the long route, playing it safe so we wouldn't be seen by Mom or Swoozie or Mrs. Mutchnick or Mr. Flatbush from Fireside Liquor, or any of the other merchants on Euclid Avenue who probably knew by now that I'd been grounded.

We headed inland again, north of downtown, up a rural road through vast farmland that gave this part of the state its reputation. Green onions grew along this road (though you'd find soybeans on the next farm road over, and citrus on the road south of town), and you could smell them from your car with the windows rolled up, which probably had something to do with why Mom and I didn't come out this way very often.

Emmett stood up to pedal and he leaned in closer to me.

"Hold on tight." He took a hard left off the road and through a break in the wire fencing, right into the onion fields, where the rows were planted so neatly and precisely that we continued on, bumping down a path dividing the crops without crushing a single one of the long, green, pungent onion stems that fluttered in the wind of our wheels.

I felt the way I had that afternoon when I'd reached Garfield Park after the hot and brush-choked climb: like I was seeing my world, the world I thought I knew every corner of, from a new perch.

"And the legend?" I called to him. "What is the legend?" I had to shout because I wasn't going to turn my head around. I believed looking forward kept me safe.

"Let's wait for that," he said. "Almost here."

We rode up to a barn surrounded by fields of green, and far enough away from the farmhouse that it was little more than a speck in the distance.

I looked at my watch.

1:19.

Emmett walked up to the large wooden door and gave three quick knocks followed by two shorter ones.

"Nobody's here," he said, and he swung the latch and pulled the barn door open. He gestured for me to follow him.

Inside the airy building were makeshift rooms divided by big sheets of brightly colored fabric hanging from the rafters.

"Jasper." He pointed to one. "Deirdre." He pointed to another. "Christian and Molly." A third. "Finn," he said as we peeked into the last. "And I'm up here." He began to climb a ladder and I followed him up to a loft where he slept with a bright orange life vest for a pillow on a bed made of straw stuffed into more of the fabric, which I recognized now. It came from the big bolts in Mrs. Mutchnick's shop. The fabric that was crowding out the summer light, that she said she had more of than she knew what to do with. She must have put it out back behind her store.

The barn wall at the head of Emmett's bed was covered in stickers. There wasn't enough room to stand, so I crawled over to take a closer look and saw that they were labels from the cheeses I'd left out. Cotswold from an English company called Royal Cheese and Dairy, port wine cheddar from Bracken Farms, a Camembert with a picture of the French flag—they were all here.

"Wow," I said, because this wall of stickers, this loft not unlike where Charlotte had gone to make her masterpiece, this barn with its fabric walls in the middle of the field of waving onion stems, it was all so unexpected. "Who owns this place?"

Emmett shrugged. "Some farmers, I guess. But they don't use the barn."

"And they don't mind that you do?"

He reached over and flattened a cheese label that was

starting to peel off at its corner. "I don't really know. But they've never come in here and told us to get lost, so I'm guessing it's okay by them. Sometimes that's the greatest kindness, the sort where you give something without showing up to get a thank-you in return." He smiled at me. "Like leaving food in a back alley."

"How'd you even find your way out here?"

"I stopped to listen to Finn play. It was a low point for me. I'd saved up all this money, I was on my way north, I was only here to change buses. But then I was attacked. Robbed of every penny. Cut with a razor blade." He put his hand to his cheek. "I thought it was over for me. That I'd have to turn back. But Finn told me not to give up, and he brought me here, and I met the others, and then, Robin, I met you."

I wanted more than anything right then to reach out and touch the spot where I'd first noticed his cut, which had now become a pale thread running the length of his left cheek. But I didn't. I was brave enough to ride on my handlebars, but not brave enough yet to throw that particular sort of caution to the wind.

He was looking at me, and I wondered whether he could feel how much I wanted to touch him.

"Better head out if we want to get back in time for your mom's phone call," he said. "And anyway, I have to tell you my favorite legend."

the legend

There was a small tribe living happily in a remote village in what is now northern California. They had everything they could hope for—bountiful food, good health, and the guidance of a benevolent Great Spirit. The chief of this tribe had two sons, whom he loved beyond measure, and the eldest of his sons was set to marry. As the tribe began to prepare for the days of celebration leading up to the wedding of the man who would one day be their chief—in times that should have been so full of happiness and glory—a terrible darkness fell upon the village. Illness struck young and old without warning. The inhabitants of this once-blessed village began to grow sick and die. The many medicines they'd relied upon in their prosperous past proved useless. The chief was at a loss for what to do, so he called upon the tribal elders.

At this meeting it was decided that there was nothing left to do but succumb to the will of the Great Spirit. If it was the Great Spirit's will that they all die, then it must be for some purpose. They would meet this fate in the brave manner for which their tribe was known.

The eldest of the elders, a wise medicine man upon whom the chief most often relied in difficult situations, stood and leaned upon his stick.

He spoke quietly and gravely. "I am an old man," he said. "And I will now tell you what my grandfather told my father when he was an old man, and what my father told me when he too was an old man. I have no son. You are all my sons. So here is what you must know. I was told that one day the Great Spirit would send a sickness to fall upon our people, and all, in turn, will die. Unless," he said, leaning more heavily on the stick, which was now shaking beneath his weight, "unless a sacrifice is made to appease the Great Spirit."

Here he averted his eyes from the chief and the chief's eldest son, their future leader, who was attending his first council of the tribal elders. "This illness will take us all, unless the firstborn son of our tribe's chief willingly gives his life for his people."

A silence fell over the group. Nothing could be heard but the crackling of the fire around which they had gathered.

The chief did not speak up in defense of his son's life. He did not need to. The rest of the assembly quickly agreed that nobody would sacrifice his life for the village. They would abide by the decision they had reached before the old medicine man had spoken, that if it was the Great Spirit's will that they all die, then they would meet their fate with bravery.

The chief's eldest son walked away from the meeting with a heavy heart. He had voted with the group, but he wasn't sure he had acted with bravery. He spoke to himself as he wandered through the woods, and he pondered both fates as he walked back into the village, where he laid eyes upon a sight that would provide a crystal-clear answer.

The face of his soon-to-be bride.

His beloved.

The face he loved more than he had words to describe was showing the first signs of the terrible illness.

That night he sat by her bedside. He held her hand. He administered the medicines that had proved useless and he mopped her brow with a cold cloth. He sat with her all the next morning and into the late afternoon, and he whispered to her that he loved her. Could she hear him? He loved her. He would always love her.

Shortly before sunset, he kissed her between her deep-set eyes. She was still alive, but he was not sure how much longer she could hold on.

He went and he found his younger brother, who, with terror in his voice, confessed that he feared he too was feeling the signs of the terrible illness.

"All will be well," the older brother said. "Be brave, and be a great leader."

The second half of this command puzzled the younger brother, but he didn't think much of it as he watched his older brother wander off into the woods. He was too consumed with worry.

The elder brother collected the largest rocks he could find and he stuffed them all into a leather sack. He dragged this sack to the edge of the boulder from which, as a boy, he loved to jump into the natural hot spring that lay hidden in the wood. This spring was believed to be a place of healing. It was where the tribe members would go to soak in the warm waters and seek cures for minor ailments—though not all believed it made any difference.

But as a boy, the eldest son had loved simply to swim there, and he had loved to dive from the boulder, and on this evening, just as the sun was setting, he took the leather bag filled with stones and he tied it to his ankle with a rope, and he held it in his arms, and he closed his eyes, and he leapt.

The next morning, the village awoke triumphant. The terrible illness was gone. Those on death's door arose from bed renewed, as if from a good night's sleep. A celebration erupted in the village, and it wasn't until all had gathered that the absence of the chief's eldest son was noticed.

The cries of the chief, and of his youngest son, and of the young woman who was no longer about to become a bride, rose up and wove together into a sound more terrible than the howling of demons.

And several days later, in a traditional ceremony, the eldest son's life was mourned and celebrated at the edge of the spring in the wood, and from that day forward nobody doubted the special healing powers of the water.

The water healed a village.

taking a leap

Back at the kitchen counter, after I'd answered Mom's two o'clock call *(Yes, I'm still here; yes, I've cleaned out the fridge; no, I'm not watching too much TV)*, Emmett told me, "I'm going to find that water."

"So . . . you're going to kill yourself? 'Cause that seems like a stupid idea."

"No, no, no. I'm not going to kill myself. God. You're so literal."

"I don't get it," I said.

"Those waters have healing powers. *Serious* healing powers. They're not like all the other hot springs, those fancy resorts where people go to, like, cure their eczema or whatever. These waters can heal *other* people. They answer prayers. That's the special thing about this spring—the water heals *others*. It's not just about the person who goes there. This water healed a village. It brought a whole tribe back from the brink of death."

I'd heard of the hot springs up north. Sometimes we'd get tourists in the shop, Germans and Brits mostly, who were making their way down the coast after a stay at one of those resorts.

And yes, maybe I was too literal, but what I understood of this legend was that the older brother had to die to save the people he loved.

"Emmett," I said, and I stopped because I could see how important this was to him. So important that he'd suffered a razor-blade cut to the cheek, so important that he'd been living in a field of onions. I didn't want to be the sort of friend who dashes dreams. Friends, I was pretty sure, lift their friends up; they don't weigh them down like a sack full of stones.

"Look," he said. "I know it sounds crazy. It does, right? But like I said, I'm looking for a *miracle*. I know. I know it's a long shot. But nothing else is working and everything is falling apart. It's already fallen apart. There's no place left to fall. My mom cries all the time. She can barely get out of bed. My dad is gone. He never calls. Or checks on us. He sends an envelope every week with five twenty-dollar bills in it and no return address. That's something, I guess, but it isn't anywhere near enough. David needs more than . . ." His voice caught and he took a long drink of his lemonade. I refilled his glass.

"All my life I've believed in that legend, Robin. At first I just believed the story. You know, like a secret history in an old dusty book. But then as things started to change, I'd lie in bed at night and imagine jumping into that spring. I could feel the warm water on my skin and I'd whisper all the prayers for healing into the dark. For David to speak and listen and understand. For my mother to stop her crying. For my father to remember what he used to love about us. I've always believed in the legend, ever since my father first read it to me, and this isn't the time to stop."

"But the sacrifice," I said. I couldn't get over that.

"But don't you see? That brother made the sacrifice, and because of what he did, those waters became what they are. I don't have to die. I just have to go there and believe. And anyway, I've made my sacrifice. Look at me. I ran away from home. I've had to hurt the people I want to heal. I know what I've done to my mother, and to David, even if he wouldn't be able to explain it. I've made sacrifices, big ones, and I have to believe that this is the spirit of the legend. I'm the firstborn son, but I don't have to die to heal my people. I know it sounds crazy, but I just have to find that spring. I have to believe. I have to stand on that boulder. And I have to take that leap."

Was he crazy? Was Emmett's believing in the healing powers of a hot spring in the woods any crazier than Finn's believing he'd find Lorelai waiting for him in Alaska? Was it any crazier than believing that if I'd gone to work that day instead of to the beach, Nick's Vespa wouldn't have hit that tree? Was it any crazier than a man of thirty-three—with a wife, a toddler, a red Fu Manchu, and a book listing all the things he still had left to do—that that man could have a heart that was all done living?

"I want to go with you," I said before I even knew what I was saying. That was the opposite of caution, wasn't it? Following the impulse of your beating heart? "I want to go to those waters."

the runaway type

We made plans for Emmett to come back the next day, in the afternoon. I wanted to go see Nick first. I needed to see him, and I was pretty sure Mom would give me a pass to leave the house in the morning. Sure, she was mad, but she'd have to see that there were more important things than being grounded.

"Okay," she said. "But only to the hospital. Then straight home again. I'll check on you at one o'clock."

"Must you treat me like a common criminal?"

"I'm just treating you the way any sane mother would treat her daughter who's beginning to try on her teenagerness. I'm showing you where the lines are. I'm reminding you what happens when you cross them."

"Fine."

"Back by one."

"Aye-aye, Captain."

So in the morning I hopped on my bike. It seemed so tame and boring riding alone on the banana seat.

On the way to the hospital I started to get cold feet. Who was I kidding? I wasn't the runaway type. I'd gone to the Safeway without leaving a note, and look where that had gotten me. I wasn't a risk taker. I wasn't a believer in miracles.

But then I thought about lists. About how one day I'd make my own book. And I wanted to have things to put in it. Things to remember. Experiences. Times I didn't take the safe route. Times I reached out and threw both arms around life.

There was so much to sort through. So many details to figure out. Emmett had done the research back in Los Angeles about how to find the hot spring in the woods. With the help of a kindly librarian who printed historical documents and maps from microfiche without charging him the five cents a page, he'd concluded that the legend had taken place near a town now known as Wilcox, in a county about two hours north of San Francisco. His librarian friend had found him a geological survey map of the area, on which there was a body of water surrounded by trees, but whether it was a hot spring or an ordinary pond he wouldn't know until he reached it. While there were hot spring resorts in the general vicinity, this body of water near what is now Wilcox was nestled amid two thousand acres of privately owned property.

It seemed like an awful lot of work had gone into this research, way beyond anything I was capable of, but it came as no surprise to me that Emmett had found someone to help him. He knew how to find people who wanted to help him. That was his special power.

Emmett knew where he had to go, but he was still saving up the money it took to get there. He'd lost everything the day he was attacked, and he was slowly building up the fare for a bus ticket to Wilcox—not an insignificant amount. He told me he'd been collecting recyclables and returning them for their deposits. He couldn't sing like Finn, but he *could* mop floors and clean grills, which he said he sometimes did for Daisy at her diner after hours. He *could* clean cages at Pacific Pets and Pet Supply. There were child labor laws, as my mother had pointed out to me that Sunday at Bartholomew's, and I guess Euclid Avenue was the kind of place where merchants took them seriously. But not so seriously that a smile and a plea from a boy with a cartoon face couldn't make them bend the rules a little.

Emmett told me that he was lucky. That he liked it here. He was happy here. And the fact that it was taking him a long time to make back the money he'd lost turned out not to be such a terrible thing.

"And anyway," he said to me, "*you* are here."

I pulled up in front of the hospital and squeezed my bike into the rack. I took off my helmet and smoothed out my hair. I didn't have my backpack with Hum inside. Poor Hum. He was grounded too. I'd left him behind on my last two adventures. The day before, I'd neglected to take him to the onion fields, because I didn't see the wisdom in us both risking a ride on the handlebars. And I might not have respected the health codes of the Cheese Shop, but hospitals were an entirely different story.

Nick was propped up in bed with a pencil and a pad of paper. His face lit up when he saw me. He still had the power to make my heart skip a beat. Corny, I know. But that's exactly what happened.

"Hey, kiddo," he said.

"Hi, Nick."

"Come on in a little closer," he said. "Give a one-legged guy a hug."

It felt good to hug him. To feel his hair on my cheek. "How's it going?"

He shrugged. He looked down at his blue hospital blanket. "You know."

"How's Becca?"

His smile widened. "She's just . . . awesome. She's at work, but she's coming by later with dinner."

"I'm so glad."

"So what's up with you, Drew? What's new in your world? How's your pasta coming along?"

He patted a spot for me to sit at the edge of his bed. I sat down facing him and he put a hand on my shin.

"I don't spend that much time at the shop anymore," I said. "And anyway, I'm grounded."

He nodded. "I think I spent my entire thirteenth year grounded."

"It's . . . I don't know. It doesn't make all that much sense. I'm kind of confused. About everything."

"Well, again, you've just described my entire thirteenth year."

I laughed.

"Nick?"

"Yeah?"

"Do you know my mom's boyfriend?"

Was that why I needed to see Nick? To press him for details about the man in the silver car?

He shook his head slowly. "C'mon, kiddo. Don't do that to me. Don't take advantage of me like that. You know I want to be your friend. You know I have a weak spot for you. But don't put me between you and your mother."

"You're right," I said. "I'm sorry."

"Forgotten."

I looked around his room. "So when are you going to get out of here?"

He sighed. "Soon, I hope. But I've got an infection they have to get under control first. And there's still more physical therapy. And I have to find a place to live that's wheelchair accessible. And there's all kinds of arrangements that have to be made, and, you know, there are days I think maybe I'd like to just stay here forever."

This was the first time Nick ever appeared to me as anything less than on top of the world, on top of a snow-covered mountain on a gloriously sunny day, and seeing this cloud pass over him as I sat on his hospital bed, I felt like weeping.

We were both quiet. I could hear carts being wheeled by in the hallway. Nurses chatting. I looked out his window at the building next door and swallowed away the urge to cry.

"Nick," I said. "Do you believe in miracles?"

I could see that he was thinking about the question. He didn't dismiss it as silly, or childish. He adjusted his pillows, propped himself up higher, and reached for the notepad he'd been writing on when I arrived.

"I want to show you something," he said. He flipped the pages back a few and held the pad out to me. "Here."

It was a sketch. Something long, wide in the middle,

narrow at the top and bottom. There were measurements and some sort of contraption in the center made from straps and bars.

It was a surfboard. A surfboard that could be ridden with only one leg.

I looked up and smiled at him.

"It's a crazy idea, I know," he said. "And that sketch is totally lame, but it's the seed of something. It's a beginning. I know I should be okay with a body board, with just lying down to surf, but I can't let go of the dream that I'll be able to stand up on a board again someday. It's the best feeling I've ever known, surfing a perfect wave, and I just can't believe that I won't ever do it again. So yes. I guess I do believe in miracles, because I believe that someday I'll stand on a surfboard and ride a perfect wave."

Whatever I'd been doing to beat back the weeping urge stopped working. Tears streamed down my face. Nick reached over for a tissue and handed it to me.

"Don't cry," he said, and a sound escaped me, a mix of a sob and a laugh. I wasn't sad, exactly. I was just flooded with all kinds of feeling.

I stood up to leave. I was running late. Mom's call would be coming in twenty minutes.

I hugged him. "Thank you."

"For what?"

I took in his smile. His sea-green eyes. His shaggy blond hair. The genuine look of concern for me.

"For being beautiful Nick."

the silver car

No matter how fast I pedaled, I wasn't going to make it home by one. I'd promised Mom that I wouldn't stop anywhere between the hospital and the house, but I figured if I swung by the Cheese Shop to tell her I was running late she'd be okay with that. I didn't think she'd consider it an infraction of her rules, though I couldn't be sure. Mom was unpredictable as of late.

I rode past the gas station and the library, past the elementary school, but instead of turning left onto Euclid Avenue, I crossed the street and turned left into the alley, the one that would lead to the parking lot behind the shop, where I'd leave my bike leaning up against Mom's car.

As soon as I pulled into the lot I saw her. I was about to call out her name when I realized she was in the middle of what looked to be a serious conversation, judging from how close she stood to the man with whom she was speaking. Then she leaned in closer and gave him a quick kiss before he climbed into his silver car. He rolled down his window. She leaned in for another kiss and then she put her palm on the roof and gave it a slap before he put the car in reverse.

She walked toward the rear door of the shop and the car backed up closer to where I stood straddling my bike, my feet part of the pavement.

As the silver car executed a three-point turn, I was able to see the driver clearly, leaving no room for doubt about his identity.

With the car safely out of sight, I managed to step back onto the pedals of my bike and continue through the alley, back onto Euclid Avenue, and all the way home, where I arrived at twelve minutes past one.

The phone was ringing as I walked in the front door.

I let it ring a few more times before I reached for it.

"Where have you been?" She sounded angry.

"The Belcher?" I asked. "Seriously, Mom? You're dating Retcher Belcher?"

A long silence followed.

"His name is Fletcher," she said. Her voice had gone from angry to controlled. Measured. She was drawing another line that I'd already started to cross.

"Ugh. Mom. I think I'm going to be sick."

"That's enough, Drew."

Another long silence.

"We'll talk more about this tonight, when I come home."

"Goodbye, Mother."

"Goodbye."

But we didn't talk that night. Mom came home after I'd

already eaten a bowl of cereal for dinner, and I told her I wasn't feeling well, and she pretended to believe me, and I went up to my room. It was a win-win situation. She didn't have to tell me the tale of how the Belcher, that meddlesome health inspector, had won her heart. And I could go upstairs and continue to convince myself that somehow she'd betrayed me.

That's how I chose to see her relationship with Fletcher Melcher, as a betrayal, because that made it easier to contemplate what I was about to do. If he was the villain out to get us all, then Mom had violated some essential trust, and if I were to go and do the same by running off with Emmett, then we'd be even. If not magical, this was certainly convenient thinking. I kept myself from reimagining Fletcher Melcher as someone who frequented our shop not because he wanted to put us out of business but because he was, understandably, so taken with my mother.

We didn't talk that night. And we didn't talk the next night because by then, I was already gone.

one last stop

Emmett and I planned to meet at the bus station. There was a bus departing for San Francisco at eleven-fifteen p.m. It would arrive at six-thirty in the morning, and we'd wait three hours for another bus, which would take us up to Wilcox. From our stop in Wilcox, according to the geological survey map Emmett would carry with him, we'd have to walk a few miles to the east to find the water in the woods.

Emmett wanted to meet me at my house. He didn't think I should ride my bike alone so late at night. I reminded him I had a reflector vest and told him it was too risky for him to come around. Better to just meet up at the bus station. That way, I'd be able to make a stop en route. One I did not want him to accompany me on.

Mom was out that night. She didn't tell me she had to work late. That ruse was over. Instead she said she was going to dinner and a movie, and that Swoozie would come over and hang out with me, which really meant *watch over* me, and I felt bad because Swoozie hadn't violated my trust but I was going to go ahead and violate hers.

She knitted. I flipped through pages of a book I wasn't really reading. We sat by the fireplace that Mom and I never lit, with Mom's Irish folk record on the stereo, and I waited for a time when I could reasonably excuse myself to go up to bed.

Finally, at nine-fifteen, I said goodnight.

"You feeling okay, Bird-girl?"

"Yeah, I'm just tired."

"You sure that's it?"

I hated to lie to Swoozie. She'd always been the one person I didn't have to keep secrets from. She listened to me. She understood me.

"Yeah, that's it. Just tired."

"Okay then." She reached for my hand and gave it a squeeze. "Sleep well."

"Thanks for keeping me company," I said.

"It's an honor and a privilege."

I went up to my room and began to pack. I couldn't take much because I needed to take Hum. I couldn't trust that when Mom realized I was gone she would remember to feed him. And anyway, what did I really need? What mattered to me other than Hum and Dad's Book of Lists, both of which I put in my backpack along with one change of clothes.

I went into Mom's room and reached under her bed. This was where she kept the foldable fire escape ladder. Though she didn't always show it, Mom was cautious too. I'd inherited that trait from her.

It was still in its package. I brought the box into my room, tore it open, and read the instructions less thoroughly than I'd have liked. My pulse was racing, and I had to get out quickly in case Swoozie decided to check on me.

I latched one end to my windowsill and dropped the rope ladder down. It unfolded soundlessly. Everything was going so much more smoothly than I expected, and before I knew it, I was in my reflector vest and helmet, pedaling up Euclid Avenue.

The afternoon before, as we'd pieced together our plan, Emmett and I had discussed how to get the money for the bus tickets. That was what had held him up this long, and now, if I was to go with him, we'd need twice as much. But I told him not to worry, that I'd take care of that. I told him I had money saved up, money given to me on various birthdays by my grandparents, and he believed me, because he didn't know that I don't have any grandparents.

I went around the back of the shop, near the Dumpster and Swoozie's smoking bench, and I used my key, the one Mom trusted me with, to open up the rear door. I crept through the office, past the walk-in freezer, up to the front counter and the cash register that I was not allowed to operate. But because one of my jobs was keeping it filled with change, I knew how to open it, and the drawer flew out toward me with a sound that made me jump.

I did feel terrible about taking the money. I told myself it wasn't stealing, because I knew that I would repay her someday. And I only took what we needed, nothing more. Just enough for two bus tickets.

I closed the register and turned to leave. But before I did I walked over to Mom's desk and sat down. I took out one of the pens she used to write checks, and I took a piece of paper.

10:25 p.m.

Dear Mom—

Before you start thinking it could have been anybody else, I want you to know that I took the money. I also want you to know that I didn't take it as payment (you never have paid me for my work here) but as a loan. One I promise to pay back as soon as I'm able.

And before you start thinking I took it for something stupid like that leather jacket you wouldn't buy me, I want you to know that I took it for something truly vital.

Please. Don't worry about me. I may be only thirteen, but I do know what I'm doing.

I will call soon. I swear I will. But I can't promise my call will arrive exactly on the hour.

Love you madly.

I went back and taped the note to the cash register, then took one last look around before locking up. I did so love the shop. In a world where some people didn't have even one place to call home, I was fortunate enough to have two.

I went out the way I'd come in and I grabbed the day-old bread and the cheese Veronica or Swoozie had left out back in the alley. I stuffed it into my bag, hopped back on my bike, and headed for the bus station.

Emmett was waiting for me out front, pacing, with his hands deep down in the pockets of his jeans. He jogged over to meet me where I'd started to place my bike in a bike rack.

"I don't have a lock," I said. With all the planning, I hadn't seen this part through. How would I keep my bike safe? Not only that, but where would I leave my helmet? My reflector vest?

"I guess we could try to find some bushes to hide it in or something."

"No," I said. "It's okay. It'll be okay." I couldn't guarantee that it wouldn't get stolen, but I figured that Emmett had made so many sacrifices to reach this point, if I had to sacrifice my bike and helmet and vest, it seemed only fair.

"You have the money?"

I patted my backpack. "Got it."

"Good, because I think I've found our father."

That had been Emmett's job. We were worried that the Greyhound agent wouldn't sell one-way tickets to Wilcox to two teenagers, no matter how mature or responsible or cautious we might have seemed. So we figured we could take the money Emmett had saved and offer it to someone at the station to pose as a parent and purchase our tickets for us.

The man Emmett picked out probably wasn't old enough to be a father to either of us. He wore a black track jacket over a T-shirt and jeans, and brand-new white tennis shoes. He was balding, unshaven, and slight. There was something entirely nonthreatening about him, which probably had something to do with why Emmett chose him, but I hoped that he wouldn't make a run for it as soon as we handed over the money, because he looked like he could run fast, like a real greyhound.

"Here you go, you crazy kids," he said as he returned from the counter with our tickets, handing one to each of us. "Ah, young love." He smiled at me. "There's nothing in the world like it."

I blushed.

"See you on board," he said, and he went over to a bench where he sat down and opened up a magazine.

"Sorry." Emmett shrugged. "I had to tell him the story I thought would work—you know, the kind that would make him want to break the rules."

"What did you say?"

"I told him we were running away together because our parents forbade us to ever see each other again. The basic Romeo and Juliet scenario."

"And that worked?"

"Yeah. The money didn't hurt either."

I looked up at the clock. Our bus would be leaving in ten minutes.

"Robin," he said, and he turned to face me. "Are you sure you're okay with this? Are you sure you want to do this? Because we can leave right now. I can go back to saving up the money on my own. I could go back to my loft in the barn for a while. As long as it takes."

I wasn't checking the clock to see if there was still time

to escape, I was checking to see how long before our adventure really began.

"I'm sure, Emmett. I'm absolutely, positively sure."

He leaned closer and shoved me a little with his shoulder. "Good. Because I am too."

let me go

The line to board the bus was longer than I'd thought it would be for a late-night departure, but that just confirmed my suspicion about where I lived: people only stopped over here, they didn't come to stay.

We stood toward the back, a few people behind our fake father. As we all stood waiting, the driver came out in his uniform and cap. He cupped his hands to his mouth.

"Ladies and gentlemen. Welcome to the eleven-fifteen to San Francisco. We will be departing shortly. Have your tickets in hand. And due to a recent security incident, we will be checking all bags prior to boarding, so please have them ready for inspection."

I felt the blood drain from my face. "Oh God. Oh no."

"What is it?" Emmett asked. He grabbed me by the elbow. "Hum," I said. I gestured to the bag on my back.

We stood and stared at each other. There was no creative thinking, no plotting left to do. The rules were clear, spelled out on a large sign above the open bus door: SHIRTS AND SHOES MUST BE WORN. ABSOLUTELY NO ALCOHOL, FIREARMS, OR ANIMALS WILL BE ALLOWED ON BOARD. WE RESERVE THE RIGHT TO REFUSE SERVICE TO ANYONE.

Emmett pulled me out of the line.

"So we can't go tonight," he said.

"We have to go tonight. There's only tonight. I'll never be able to do this again."

He led me out of the terminal, outside onto the street. I filled my lungs with the cool night air.

It was because of Hum that I was here; he'd brought me to Emmett. He'd delivered me to this moment. Mrs. Mutchnick had handed him to me that night of the grand opening because I looked like I needed a friend. And now I had one. A real friend.

I put my bag down on the sidewalk and unzipped it. I took Hum out of his cage. He made his happy clicking sound. I scratched him behind his ears. I'd thought he had no wisdom to impart, that he wasn't magical, that he couldn't talk, but as I looked at him, I could almost hear him whisper: *Let me go*.

It was one thing to sacrifice my bike, but this was my Hum. His Excellency the Lord High Rat Humboldt Fog. I couldn't imagine a world without him. How could I let him go?

I turned around and looked back inside the terminal. Half of the line had already boarded the bus. The time to choose was running out.

"Robin," Emmett said, and then he stopped. There was nothing left to say.

I walked around the side of the building to a cluster of trees and a stretch of unmowed grass. Emmett followed.

I got down onto my knees. I took out a macadamia nut and held it in my outstretched palm. Hum devoured it quickly and I took out another.

"Humboldt Fog," I said. "You are an excellent rat."

Tears welled in my eyes and fell onto the grass.

"If you can understand me, hear this: I will come back for you, but it's okay if you don't wait around for me. It's okay if you go on and find another life for yourself. You are a good rat. A kind rat. And maybe you'll be a happier rat when you discover that the world is bigger than your little wire cage."

I reached out and I touched him one more time. Just under his chin. And then I took the macadamia nut, and I threw it as far as I could into the grass, and I watched him run off after it, just like Emmett had taught him to do.

I grabbed Emmett by the arm and pulled him toward the station doors. I didn't look back to see if Hum was playing out his role in our little game of fetch—if he was returning to me, the nut clenched in his teeth. I didn't look back, so that someday, when I remembered this moment, I might be able to picture Hum picking up the nut, and then continuing to run, happily, far away through the tall grass.

awake and alive

As the bus took us north on a connection of dark farm roads and smaller highways, I started to wonder where all the cars were. How could the streets be so empty? How could people sleep when there was so much at stake, so much happening, when there were so many reasons to be awake and alive?

And I wondered how it was that I could feel both empty, like these streets, and yet so full at the same time. And those weren't the only contrasting poles inside me. I felt sad and happy. Scared and exhilarated. I felt young and old.

I leaned my forehead against the window. It was cold against my skin.

We didn't say anything to each other for a very long time.

Finally, Emmett spoke. "I'm sorry," he said. "I'm so, so sorry."

I kept my face to the window. *Hum. My Hum.*

He put his hand on my shoulder. "Are you going to be okay?"

I turned to him. "I think so."

"I hope this all turns out to be worth it," he said. "I hope this isn't just a big waste."

I hoped so too. I hoped that Emmett was right to believe in the waters and that I was wrong to have my doubts. I hoped so, but in a way, I didn't care what was real and what was just a crazy dream. How could I tell Emmett that this was already the most important thing that had ever happened to me? That it didn't matter if the legend was true? That I'd already taken my leap? I'd risked everything, and I felt alive. Just sitting here with him on this midnight bus in the dark was worth everything I'd given up and more.

I couldn't tell him any of this because Emmett believed in the waters. He had to believe in the waters. His life depended upon it. And because of that, because he was my friend, I wanted to believe in them too. I wanted to believe that we were on a journey that was only beginning, and that when we finally reached our destination, we'd be able to heal our people.

And so I believed. I began to think about the people in my life who needed healing. I leaned back in my seat and I tilted my head away from the coldness of the window, closer to Emmett, and I imagined easing the pain of the people I loved, and I let the rocking bus, and the darkness, and the empty roads draw me in to sleep.

the magician's party trick

Emmett woke me with a gentle nudge.

I looked out my window. Exhaust still poured from our pipes and the pipes of the buses on either side of us. Gone were the vast fields of farmland, the empty roads, and the darkness. We idled just outside the terminal, a concrete block with yesterday's trash strewn on the surrounding sidewalks, under a large and very noisy overpass.

To me, it was almost unspeakably beautiful. Here I was, in San Francisco, at the break of day. Dad's favorite place.

I turned to Emmett and smiled. "Good morning."

"Right back at you."

We were the last to disembark from the bus, and as all the other passengers hustled off in various directions, we stood for a minute, not knowing what to do or where to go.

We had three hours to kill.

"I'm sorry I didn't bring more money," I said. "I wish I

could take us to breakfast. There must be a diner somewhere, someplace like Daisy's."

He threw his arms out wide and spun around. "Who wants to go sit in a diner? Look where we are. Have you ever been here?"

"I've never been anywhere."

"So then, let me show you around."

"You've been?"

"No. But I'm a really good tour guide."

He linked his arm through mine and we found our way down to the water, which is almost an inevitability in San Francisco. Three of the four directions we could have walked in would have brought us to the water.

We wandered past huge docks with enormous boats. Everything was arriving and departing, coming and going, just like I'd always imagined about home. Even Emmett and me—we were here now but we'd be gone soon—and it felt, at that moment, like the only way to be in the world.

The sky lightened slowly, from metal-gray to dolphin-gray, and it was cooler than I'd expected, with a wind that made me tighten my arm in his, drawing him closer.

"What do you think of when you think of San Francisco?" he asked. *Dad.* I thought of Dad, but that's not what I said.

"Rice-A-Roni?"

He laughed. "No, I mean, what do you picture when you close your eyes and imagine the city?"

"I guess . . . the Golden Gate Bridge?"

He separated himself from me and looked at his watch. "Then I'm going to show you the Golden Gate Bridge. C'mon, let's pick up the pace."

We continued to walk with the water to our right. We went by more docks and piers. We passed hotels and people wandering into and out of coffee shops. Garbage trucks rumbled by. Seagulls screamed at each other. The salty air was thick with morning fog.

"How do you know where we're going?"

"Well, for one, we've got a pretty decent chance of finding a bridge if we stick close to the water. And two, I know my maps. And I know the Golden Gate Bridge is at the mouth of the bay. The city's northern tip." He motioned straight ahead. "This direction."

Eventually our path wound up a hill in a park with a collection of red-roofed buildings. We walked through a tunnel of trees, climbing until we reached the crest, and there it was before us: half of the Golden Gate Bridge.

I could see the red pillars reaching up out of the water, and the cars moving slowly through the morning traffic, but the rest of the bridge, the tall twin ladders and cables that inspired songs and poetry, were covered in a heavy blanket of fog.

We sat on a park bench and I started to make us sandwiches out of the cheese and bread from the alley. Whoever had left it had also left some marinated artichokes and red peppers, and I couldn't understand how any of this wasn't good enough to sell. We ate in silence, watching the bridge.

And then, magically, the upper half began to materialize, as if from thin air. First faint and blurred, like a watercolor painting, and then strong and vibrant, an electric red against a pale blue sky.

Right then, I put it on my list.

Most Memorable Moments: *watching the Golden Gate Bridge appear like a magician's party trick.*

"I want to show you something." I took out Dad's Book of Lists and handed it to him. He began to flip through it. Letting him see this book, I felt like Hum when he'd roll over and display his belly. *We are friends*, this move of Hum's told me. *I trust you.*

"This is amazing," he said. "You're so lucky to have this."

"I know."

"You're so, so lucky he left this for you."

"Do you think he left it for me? I've wondered. I've wondered if he wrote these lists so I could read them."

Emmett looked at me with one eyebrow raised. "My father didn't leave anything. Not even an address. He doesn't seem to care if I know him, and he's getting his wish, because I'm already starting to forget him. But your dad"—Emmett placed the book back into my hands—"he wanted you to know him."

I stared at the black-and-white-static cover, the dots swarming before my eyes. I felt myself slipping into a place of grief and sorrow, but then Emmett checked his watch, jumped up, and grabbed me by the arm.

"If we don't run, *now*," he said, and for the first time I heard panic in his voice, "we're going to miss our bus."

We ran along the water's edge of a city much more awake. We wove in and out of the crowds at Fisherman's Wharf and the clusters of men with briefcases arriving on the ferries from the other side of the bay.

I had no idea how to find the bus terminal again, but

Emmett led us back through the city streets. We ran harder now, and though it violated every rule I held dear, we crossed traffic against red lights. We reached the doors just as they were about to close.

We climbed on board and collapsed into our seats, and by the time we'd caught our breath, we were under those ladders and cables, sailing over the Golden Gate Bridge.

We started walking up the road. It felt like we walked a hundred miles, undoubtedly because, as Mom loved to point out, I didn't get much exercise. Eventually we veered right onto an unpaved road. We walked by houses and farms; everything so spread apart you had to wonder why people needed that much land. Could you know your neighbors, know your community, when so much space divided you?

"It's looking like it's farther than I thought," Emmett said, scowling at his map. We stopped underneath the shade of a tree with a wispy trunk and a full canopy of tiny green leaves. We drank from our bottles. In the distance I saw cows, big and deep brown. Mean-looking cows I was happy were kept to their side of the road by a wooden fence.

"We've got to make it by sunset. That's when we have to take the plunge. As the sun is setting, just like in the legend." He looked up at the sky. "We've still got time."

I was tired. I hadn't had much sleep. And like the way revelations sometimes came to me in the haze just before losing consciousness, something occurred to me.

"Emmett," I said. "You're a terrible swimmer."

He looked at me.

"You told me so that day on the beach. At the cove. Sitting on the surfboard table. You asked me to teach you to swim."

"That's right," he said. "I'm a terrible swimmer."

"So what do you plan to do?"

He gave me the signature Emmett look. The *how could you ask such an obvious question* look. "Hold on to you."

"But what if I hadn't come? What if you'd been alone? What if I wasn't here?"

you are here

Though Emmett's research told him Wilcox was only two and a half hours north of San Francisco, the bus ride took us five. That's what happens when you get on a bus to nowhere.

Our trip took us by vineyards and factories, up hills and through valleys, past bars with dilapidated porches and signs promising ninety-nine-cent beers, and white clapboard churches. We drove through towns with fancy-looking restaurants and towns with nothing but a gas station and a hardware store.

It's not like there aren't major highways north of San Francisco—in fact, there's one that would have taken us there in exactly half the time—but there's no such thing as a direct bus to Wilcox.

We had hours to talk, and Emmett told me about his brother. If chasing this legend wasn't proof enough of how much he loved the kid, it was there in the way he said his name. *David*. The way his eyes lit up and his cartoon smile grew bigger.

When we fell silent, I watched the green hills and thought about Mom. I imagined her hair puffed out from the way she pulled on it in times of trouble. I imagined her pacing. Unable to sit. Unable to eat. I imagined her thin frame wrapped in Swoozie's embrace. I even imagined her leaning into Fletcher Melcher as he draped an arm over her shoulder, and the thought didn't make me ill, it made me feel happy for her.

I closed my eyes and tried to send her some peace. I tried sending her a telepathic message, through whatever fine thread still connected us, that I was okay. I was safe. *Don't worry, Mom. I can take care of myself.*

"Wilcox!" the driver called out. "This here's Wilcox!"

I don't know what I'd expected, but I'd expected more than this: a long empty road interrupted only by Gus's General Store, with a bench out front that served as the bus stop.

Needless to say, nobody was waiting on that bench. There was nobody as far as the eye could see. We'd have missed Wilcox altogether if the driver hadn't bellowed its name.

We thanked him and climbed off the bus.

He nodded. "Good luck." He pulled the lever and the doors closed behind us with a loud sigh.

What had made him say that? Did we look like we needed some luck? Were hope and desperation written all over our faces? Our tired bodies? Our half-empty backpacks?

We sat on the bench and Emmett took out his map and a compass.

I looked longingly at Gus's General Store. What I wouldn't

have done for a Good News bar. Instead I reached for w was left of the French bread and broke it in half.

"It's a good five miles if this map can be trusted. Ma more." Emmett tore at the bread with his teeth. It had g from day-old to almost-two-day-old. Hard as a rock.

"At least it's pretty here," I said.

Bushes bloomed with dusty rose-colored flowers, l and soft like feathers. The farmland and the hillsides w every shade of green, from a light almost-yellow to the d green of forests. A bird flew overhead, all black save fo shock of red at the crests of both its wings, and you could hear a sound beyond the rushing of a nearby creek. Otl than the fact that we were far from the ocean, it wasn't a d matically different landscape from the Central Coast, there was beauty to me in the fact that I was somewhere never been.

I tilted my face to the sun. I let it warm me.

"Do you think Gus might find it in his heart to fill up o water bottles?" Emmett asked.

"Maybe. If we smile real pretty at him."

"That should be easy enough for you," he said, and I fe my face go from warm to hot.

Inside it smelled of burnt coffee. Gus wasn't Gus but teenage girl named Lila, who wore cutoff jean shorts, a plai flannel shirt, and the specific sort of boredom that belonge to long summer days devoid of human contact. She filled ou bottles from a tap in the back.

We thanked her and she shrugged, not seeming particu larly interested in or curious about what we were up to, two strangers in a town where she probably knew everyone.

you are here

Though Emmett's research told him Wilcox was only two and a half hours north of San Francisco, the bus ride took us five. That's what happens when you get on a bus to nowhere.

Our trip took us by vineyards and factories, up hills and through valleys, past bars with dilapidated porches and signs promising ninety-nine-cent beers, and white clapboard churches. We drove through towns with fancy-looking restaurants and towns with nothing but a gas station and a hardware store.

It's not like there aren't major highways north of San Francisco—in fact, there's one that would have taken us there in exactly half the time—but there's no such thing as a direct bus to Wilcox.

We had hours to talk, and Emmett told me about his brother. If chasing this legend wasn't proof enough of how much he loved the kid, it was there in the way he said his name. *David*. The way his eyes lit up and his cartoon smile grew bigger.

When we fell silent, I watched the green hills and thought about Mom. I imagined her hair puffed out from the way she pulled on it in times of trouble. I imagined her pacing. Unable to sit. Unable to eat. I imagined her thin frame wrapped in Swoozie's embrace. I even imagined her leaning into Fletcher Melcher as he draped an arm over her shoulder, and the thought didn't make me ill, it made me feel happy for her.

I closed my eyes and tried to send her some peace. I tried sending her a telepathic message, through whatever fine thread still connected us, that I was okay. I was safe. *Don't worry, Mom. I can take care of myself.*

"Wilcox!" the driver called out. "This here's Wilcox!"

I don't know what I'd expected, but I'd expected more than this: a long empty road interrupted only by Gus's General Store, with a bench out front that served as the bus stop.

Needless to say, nobody was waiting on that bench. There was nobody as far as the eye could see. We'd have missed Wilcox altogether if the driver hadn't bellowed its name.

We thanked him and climbed off the bus.

He nodded. "Good luck." He pulled the lever and the doors closed behind us with a loud sigh.

What had made him say that? Did we look like we needed some luck? Were hope and desperation written all over our faces? Our tired bodies? Our half-empty backpacks?

We sat on the bench and Emmett took out his map and a compass.

I looked longingly at Gus's General Store. What I wouldn't

have done for a Good News bar. Instead I reached for what was left of the French bread and broke it in half.

"It's a good five miles if this map can be trusted. Maybe more." Emmett tore at the bread with his teeth. It had gone from day-old to almost-two-day-old. Hard as a rock.

"At least it's pretty here," I said.

Bushes bloomed with dusty rose-colored flowers, long and soft like feathers. The farmland and the hillsides were every shade of green, from a light almost-yellow to the dark green of forests. A bird flew overhead, all black save for a shock of red at the crests of both its wings, and you couldn't hear a sound beyond the rushing of a nearby creek. Other than the fact that we were far from the ocean, it wasn't a dramatically different landscape from the Central Coast, but there was beauty to me in the fact that I was somewhere I'd never been.

I tilted my face to the sun. I let it warm me.

"Do you think Gus might find it in his heart to fill up our water bottles?" Emmett asked.

"Maybe. If we smile real pretty at him."

"That should be easy enough for you," he said, and I felt my face go from warm to hot.

Inside it smelled of burnt coffee. Gus wasn't Gus but a teenage girl named Lila, who wore cutoff jean shorts, a plaid flannel shirt, and the specific sort of boredom that belonged to long summer days devoid of human contact. She filled our bottles from a tap in the back.

We thanked her and she shrugged, not seeming particularly interested in or curious about what we were up to, two strangers in a town where she probably knew everyone.

We started walking up the road. It felt like we walked a hundred miles, undoubtedly because, as Mom loved to point out, I didn't get much exercise. Eventually we veered right onto an unpaved road. We walked by houses and farms; everything so spread apart you had to wonder why people needed that much land. Could you know your neighbors, know your community, when so much space divided you?

"It's looking like it's farther than I thought," Emmett said, scowling at his map. We stopped underneath the shade of a tree with a wispy trunk and a full canopy of tiny green leaves. We drank from our bottles. In the distance I saw cows, big and deep brown. Mean-looking cows I was happy were kept to their side of the road by a wooden fence.

"We've got to make it by sunset. That's when we have to take the plunge. As the sun is setting, just like in the legend." He looked up at the sky. "We've still got time."

I was tired. I hadn't had much sleep. And like the way revelations sometimes came to me in the haze just before losing consciousness, something occurred to me.

"Emmett," I said. "You're a terrible swimmer."

He looked at me.

"You told me so that day on the beach. At the cove. Sitting on the surfboard table. You asked me to teach you to swim."

"That's right," he said. "I'm a terrible swimmer."

"So what do you plan to do?"

He gave me the signature Emmett look. The *how could you ask such an obvious question* look. "Hold on to you."

"But what if I hadn't come? What if you'd been alone? What if I wasn't here?"

He reached over and took a strand of my hair that had fallen into my face and tucked it behind my ear, just like my mother always did, though it felt entirely different.

"But you *are* here," he said. "I had a life vest, but I didn't bring it. I don't need it. Because you are here."

hold on tight

By the time we reached the edge of the land that held the miracle waters, it was closer to sunset than Emmett wanted it to be. I could tell by his quicker pace and the way he kept drumming his fingers on his thigh.

We walked along the perimeter of the fence looking for a break where we could enter without sacrificing our flesh to the layers of barbed wire. We finally found a wooden gate the owners must have used to enter on foot or horseback. The gate and the path it opened onto were too narrow for any vehicle.

It was locked, of course. And there was a sign:

NO TRESPASSING. VIOLATORS WILL BE PROSECUTED TO THE FULL EXTENT OF THE LAW. THAT MEANS YOU.

I was already facing prosecution beyond what I could possibly fathom—my mother's law was greater than the law of the land—so this sign intimidated me less than I'd have expected.

My long legs came in handy as Emmett hoisted me up and over the gate. He followed. Here we were, finally. Off the roads. On the land. Somewhere near the birthplace of legend.

Emmett stared at his compass. He stared at his map. His eyes darted back and forth between the two and then he started off on the path, through the tall grass dotted with wildflowers.

The sun was already starting to slip behind the hills in front of us, but that was only because the hills were high; there was still some time left before real dark.

We wandered through open fields; we climbed up those hills and then down again. We walked in and out of the shade of trees. We even had to wade across a creek. I let my mind go completely. Following was liberating. Trusting someone else. Relinquishing control.

Finally, Emmett stopped. We were on a path that looked familiar, just around a bend in the hillside, but I thought that was only because to me, so much nature starts to look the same after a while.

"We're walking in circles," he said. He crumpled up his map and threw it. It didn't go very far. "I don't know what I'm doing. We're so close, and I don't know how to find it." He sat down on a fallen tree, and I sat next to him.

He put his head in his hands. "I don't know what I'm doing."

I wanted to ask if maybe there was a chance that the hot spring didn't exist. That the kindly librarian and all her microfiche had been wrong. But I remembered the sack of stones. I didn't want to be the one to sink him. I wanted to be his life vest.

I put my hand gently on his shoulder. We watched the sky turn one small notch farther on the dial toward black.

And then: the sound of footfalls. I braced for a large animal to turn the bend and discover us, maybe one of those angry-looking cows, but instead it was a man. Tall and slim, with heavy hiking boots, a gray mustache, and dark sunglasses.

"Hey," he said. "Hey, you kids!" He started walking faster toward us, and I found myself wishing it had been a cow, because I was pretty sure we could outrun a cow. There was no way we could outrun this hostile-looking man.

We stood up.

"Can't you read? This is *private property*. You are on *my* private property."

"I'm sorry, sir," Emmett said. "I guess we're lost."

"Lost on my side of a barbed-wire fence? I don't think so. You're on my land. And this is my path, where I like to take my afternoon walk and not have to talk to anybody. You are officially ruining my day."

He took off his sunglasses and placed them in his shirt pocket. He became less menacing as soon as I could see his pale gray eyes.

He put his hands on his hips. "So what did you come for? Huh? My Mexican avocadoes? To have some fun with my livestock? Or are you looking for a spot to drink beer where your folks won't find you?"

"None of that," I said.

"So?"

I looked at Emmett. He'd been keeping his secrets so long I don't think it occurred to him to tell the truth. I nodded to him. *Go ahead. Tell him. Tell him why we're here.*

"We're looking for a hot spring," Emmett said, staring at his sneakers. "From a legend my father used to read me. Waters. Miracle waters that healed a village."

The man let out a deep sigh.

"Oh, that."

Maybe we weren't the first kids who'd run away to look for miracles on his land. Maybe it was our turn, and tomorrow there'd be more just like us. Maybe everyone was looking for a miracle.

"You're not too far off," he said. "West. You need to keep west. Go back down this path to the valley floor. Follow the creek. Soon enough, you'll be able to smell it."

Emmett looked up at this man, whose posture had softened considerably.

"So it's true? The waters *are* here? The ones from the legend?"

"That's what they tell me, son."

"And is it true? Do they work? Are they miracle waters?"

He scratched at his mustache. "I can't say. All you can do is go and find out for yourself. So go on. Get off my walking path. Follow the creek. Find the hot spring. And then, after you do, please be kind enough to leave my property."

"Yes, sir," Emmett said. "Thank you."

The man nodded and took a few steps ahead of us, where he bent down to pick up Emmett's crumpled map like he was collecting a thoughtlessly discarded candy wrapper. He tucked it under his arm and continued around another bend in the path, out of sight.

We started to run. Back down the hillside to the valley floor. We ran along the side of the creek. We ran west, chasing the slipping sun.

I hadn't had time to consider what the man meant when he said soon enough we'd smell it, but out of this valley of wildflowers and blossoming trees came the scent of rotten eggs. Strong enough to stop us in our tracks.

"Wow. What died?" I held the sleeve of my sweatshirt up to cover my nose.

Emmett took in a deep, greedy breath. He broke into a grin.

"Sulfur," he said. "We must be close."

And we were. In front of us, a dense cluster of trees, gathered as if protecting something. Something that the world might eat up whole. And no more than a hundred paces into these trees we came upon the spring. Steam rising from the dark waters. A boulder to the side. A place from which to leap.

It was smaller and less majestic than I'd imagined. I think I'd confused my fantasies of visiting Hawaii with finding these waters; I'd convinced myself that this faraway place I longed to reach would be like something on a postcard. But the creek and the wildflower-strewn valley were far lovelier than this dark, smelly, steaming, watery hole, sheltered in a knot of tangled trees.

Emmett's eyes brimmed with tears.

"This is it," he whispered. He kicked off his shoes. He took off his shirt. Even in this moment, I was able to admire the smoothness of his skin, tight over the muscles just starting to push their way out of his lanky torso. The patch of hair underneath each of his armpits.

The smell of his sweat mixed with the smell of sulfur. It was an earthy, natural smell. The smell of life.

He scrambled to the top of the boulder.

He looked down at me and reached out his hand.

I sat and unlaced my shoes. I took care removing my sweatshirt and the long-sleeved T-shirt I wore over a tank top. I folded them both neatly and placed them next to my balled up socks. I proceeded slowly, with caution, not for the sake of caution itself, but because I wanted this moment to last forever.

I rolled up my jeans to my knees.

I climbed up the boulder and stood next to Emmett and I took hold of his outstretched hand.

"Thank you," he said to me. "A million times, thank you." He wiped at his eyes with his free hand. "I wouldn't be here without you."

"Don't forget," I said. "Hold on tight."

He nodded.

We stood like that for a minute. Squeezing each other's hands. His eyes were clenched shut. He was concentrating. He was praying. Hoping. Dreaming. He was begging for his miracle.

I closed my eyes too.

I pictured Nick in his hospital bed. His surfboard sketch. I thought of Swoozie and all the love in each embrace. I thought of Mom and her closet of sweaters and the secrets she hid there. Her calculator ribbon. Her ledger book. Her blossoming romance. Her life. I thought of my own life. The start of eighth grade. The ways I might begin again. Find real friends.

Though I didn't know him, I thought of David. Of Emmett's father. His mother. I imagined them together. Happy. I heard the faintest sound of laughter.

Emmett squeezed my hand tighter. I opened my eyes. He was looking at me.

"Are you ready?"

I nodded. "Ready."

"I'll hold on. I won't forget."

We stepped to the edge of the boulder. We took a long look at each other.

And then we leapt.

epilogue

I'm guessing that when you think back on your first kiss, it doesn't involve a 76 station on the side of Interstate 5, the sound of passing eighteen-wheelers, and the glare of four eyes belonging to two angry mothers. But that is where my very first kiss happened. This wasn't even a *real* first kiss, as it didn't involve my lips. Emmett kissed me between my eyes, just like the boy in the legend did to his soon-to-be bride as she clung to life, a kiss to say don't leave me, don't slip away, I will make everything right.

It also turned out to be a kiss goodbye. It was the last I would ever see of him.

I thought he might kiss me as we sat shivering on the bank of the spring with our clothes soaked through and our feet dangling in the steaming water. We looked into each other's eyes the way I'd always imagined people did right before they leaned in closer and touched lips for the first time.

But that was all we did. We looked at each other. Into each other. We were still clutching hands.

When we finally walked out of the woods that night, cold, damp, and unsure of what we had done, of whether any of the miracles we shut our eyes and dared hope for might come true, it was late. The sky was dark and full of stars. I was tired and hungry and stinking of sulfur. I felt profoundly happy.

At Gus's General Store Lila helped me place a call to my mother, who unleashed a whiplash-inducing array of reactions. But the strongest sound in her voice was relief. I was safe. My phone call spelled the end of her worst nightmare.

She asked me for Emmett's home number. She said no mother should ever have to go through what she'd been through over the past twenty-four hours. I cupped my hand over the phone and asked him. He took a pen from the store's countertop and wrote it on my palm. I read it aloud to my mother.

"Don't move a muscle," she said. "I'll be there as fast as humanly possible." She hung up, dialed the number I'd given her, climbed into her car, and drove through the night.

Lila gave us cans of soda and slabs of beef jerky and some Kraft spreadable cheese that came with little red sticks and stale crackers. Eventually she had to lock up and go home, and she left us out front, on the bench, with a few blankets she found in the storage room to protect ourselves against the creeping cold.

My mother pulled up around three in the morning. She didn't turn off the headlights or close her door. She jumped out with the ignition still running and raced over to me and pulled me into her. She leaned back and looked at my face. She stroked my cheek. She reached over to Emmett and she touched him too, because despite everything, he was still a boy and she was still a mother.

"Get into the car," she said angrily, but then, in an act of kindness, she opened the back door for us both. She might not have understood why, but she knew that we'd need this last time together. To sit next to each other with our legs touching, listening to each other breathing. Emmett reached over and he took my hand again, and he didn't let go for the entire five hours it took to reach the interstate turnoff halfway between San Francisco and Los Angeles, where Mom had arranged to meet his mother.

After the sad, silent wave we gave each other as we climbed into cars that would drive us in opposite directions, Mom didn't say a word to me. Talk would come later. Fury and scolding, about how I'd aided and abetted a fugitive. Questioning, about whether I'd let him do things to me that I wasn't ready for. Reprimanding, about the way I'd put myself in danger. Reminding, about how the world was an unsafe place I wasn't yet old enough to navigate without her guidance.

And then, finally, understanding, when she was able to stop talking and really listen to why I'd run away. Why, after being such a reliable kid for so long, I'd gone and done something so reckless. So crazy. So completely irrational.

Because, I told her, I wanted to believe.

Every day for the first two weeks after getting back home I went to the bus station to look for Hum. I'd bring along a bag of macadamia nuts and sit in the grass, throwing one after the other after the other, waiting for him to come bounding toward me with one of those nuts between his teeth. He never did, and eventually I stopped going to the bus station.

Emmett's number remained on my palm for days—it turned out to be a permanent marker he'd reached for that night—but I never called him. I never did for the same reason I stopped going to the bus station to look for Hum.

It was easier to invent my own ending, like the way Mom had always told me my father's heart stopped working, that he was *all done living,* so that I wouldn't have to know that he died in fear and in pain of a disease that ravaged his young body in a matter of months.

I chose to imagine that Hum had found a better life. To imagine that David could hear and understand and even laugh at Emmett's stories of Conan the Barbarian, that their father returned to live with the family, and that come the following spring, they would plant a cucumber patch in their backyard.

I chose to believe in miracles.

I'm eighteen now, and soon I'll be able to see that magician's trick, the sudden appearance of the Golden Gate Bridge on any day I choose. The University of California at Berkeley is across a different bridge, but San Francisco is close enough that I can go into the city whenever I like, and I can take that walk, and find that bench, and tear into a piece of bread. Something tells me I'll do that often.

My mother still owns her shop on Euclid Avenue. She was ahead of her time, and the rest of the world finally caught up with her. The Cheese Shop is now one of several gourmet stores in town doing a thriving business, but you can ask any-body. They'll tell you hers is the best by far.

She lives in the same small house by the beach, but she's threatening to turn my room into her yoga studio where no-body will be allowed, not even her husband, Fletch, to whom I must officially apologize for the way I thought the worst of him when I didn't know him at all. He has been nothing short of wonderful to her, as he was to me, during the not-always-easy years of my adolescence.

Nick finally made it to college, but it took another year to fill out those applications. He returned to work and Mom rode him until I think he did it just to shut her up, and when he went, he put an ocean between them. He and Becca will graduate from the University of Hawaii next May, and they plan to stay in Honolulu, where they hope to open up a surf shop one day. Nick has yet to perfect his one-legged surfboard, though not for lack of trying. Occa-sionally he'll send me a package with a box of Good News bars, since Hawaii is the only place left where you can get them.

I can't believe I've never been to visit. I still dream of going to Hawaii, and I know I will, someday.

Miracles happen slowly. Not overnight. Not with a leap from a boulder, or a plunge into hot water.

There are the days when I think I don't believe anymore. When I think I've grown too old for miracles. And that's right when another one seems to happen.

Like today, when I looked into the mailbox and found his letter.

It had no return address, though as soon as I opened it, I knew it was from Emmett. I reached inside the envelope and pulled out a perfectly folded paper crane.

It took a while, but I want you to know that because of you, things are better.
So, thank you.
For feeding me.
For helping me find where I was going.
For letting go of something you loved so dearly so you could come along with me.
For holding my hand and saving me from drowning.

If I could make my own paper bird and send it out into the world so that it might find its way to him, or if those numbers hadn't washed from my palm all those years ago, I would pick up the phone and call him.

Can you hear me, Emmett Crane?

You were my first real friend, the first person I really knew, who knew me too, so it doesn't surprise me that I want to say to you the very same things you said to me.

Thank you.

You saved me from drowning.

Because of you, things are better.

Dana Reinhardt lives in San Francisco with her husband and their two daughters. She is the author of *The Things a Brother Knows*, *How to Build a House*, *Harmless*, and *A Brief Chapter in My Impossible Life*. Visit her on the Web at danareinhardt.net.